Kindred Spirits

D1264552

Julia Watts

2008
bean pole books

Beanpole Books
P.O. Box 242
Midway, Florida 32343

Printed in the United States of America on acid-free paper
First Edition

Editor: Katherine V. Forrest
Cover designer: Kiaro Creative Ltd.

ISBN 10: 0-9667359-9-4
ISBN 13: 978-0-9667359-9-4

For Ian and Alec

Acknowledgments

My thanks go to all "the usual suspects," especially Carol and Don and my mom and dad. I am especially grateful to the divine Katherine V. Forrest for her brilliant editing and to Linda Hill and Sara Joyce for welcoming me into the Beanpole Books family.

About the Author

Julia Watts is the author of the Lambda Literary Award-winning young-adult novel *Finding H.F.* as well as several novels for adult readers. She lives with her family in Knoxville, Tennessee, in a house full of books and cats.

Chapter One

I don't know why Mom bothers to buy candy at Halloween because we never get any trick-or-treaters. Not even one.

Not that I'm complaining. Right now I'm on my eighth miniature Hershey Bar. No point in letting good chocolate go to waste.

"Miranda," Mom says, checking for the millionth time that the porch light is on, "don't eat all the candy. You'll rot out your teeth, and besides, it's early. Some kids could still show up."

"Mom, nobody's coming, and you know it."

Mom looks out the window. A half a dozen kids dressed as ghosts and witches and cartoon characters run past our house like demons are chasing them. Even from inside the house we can hear their screams. "You're right," Mom says. "Pass me some of that candy, will you?"

Part of the reason trick-or-treaters stay away is our house. We live in a big, two-story house built in 1892. Like a lot of houses built back then, it's fancy, with gingerbread trim on the porch posts and a tower overlooking the front yard. Of course, what I call fancy is what a lot of other people call spooky, especially since the house is painted dark plum (my mom's color choice) and has a peach tree in the front yard which is bursting with white blossoms in the spring, but is bare and gnarled and witchy-looking by the time Halloween rolls around.

I'd like to say the house and the tree are the only reasons people stay away on Halloween and on every other night of the year, but that would be a lie. The main reason is us.

"Us" is Granny, Mom, and me. Let's just say that the three of us aren't exactly the most popular gals in Wilder, Kentucky.

Don't get me wrong. Granny and Mom are the best-hearted women you could hope to meet, and I'm a pretty good girl most of the time. But folks here don't trust us maybe because Wilder is way back in the mountains and is populated by just over a thousand people who are suspicious of anybody who's the least bit different than they are.

Granny and Mom and I are different. Real different. Some of it's the way we look. Granny is stooped and wrinkled and has silver hair long enough to sit on, which she wears in a braid down her back. The only color she ever wears is black. She even dyes her nightgowns black. Mom, though, likes to wear bright colors and loud prints and lots of big, jangly jewelry. She wouldn't look out of place in a big city, but here she sticks out like a peacock in a chicken coop.

And me, I dress in clothes that Mom sews for me instead of the latest styles from the Young Miss shop the next town over, and my hair is a big cloud of curls the color of a new copper penny.

My eyes are the same shade of green as a cat's. Granny and Mom think my eyes are beautiful, but the kids at school think they're spooky.

But our looks aren't really why people are afraid of us. The reason goes back years and years.

When Granny was my age, she thought little Wilder was the big city. She was raised in the backwoods by her ma, who was a widow. They lived in a two-room shack and scraped by on the money Granny's ma made from picking herbs and cooking them up into potions she sold that could cure anything from an upset stomach to a broken heart.

Granny's ma was different like Granny and Mom and me are. The women in my family have always had the same kind of difference. Granny calls it the Sight.

Granny says she discovered she had the Sight when she was just six years old. Her ma was hanging clothes on the line when Granny said to her, "We've got to get the chickens out of the chicken coop." Granny didn't know why they had to do it, she says; she just knew they had to. Her ma rigged up a pen in the yard and put the chickens in it, and that night the chicken coop burned to the ground.

Granny was scared that her ma would think that she had set the fire herself, but her ma said, "I know you didn't set that fire, Irene. You just knowed that the chickens would be in danger if we didn't get them out of the coop. You've got the Sight, honey. Just like me and my ma and her ma before her. It's a gift."

Granny stayed at home with her and learned how to boil down plants into healing teas and syrups and tinctures. She learned how to tell people's fortunes by looking at the leaves in the bottom of their tea cup or by having them open up the Bible to a certain verse. After Granny's ma died, she took over her ma's work, making potions, telling fortunes, and curing boils and sties.

She didn't meet my grandfather until she was forty years old and he showed up on her doorstep with a bullet stuck in his arm from a hunting accident. Once Granny found out that he worked for the coal company and so didn't need to hunt in order to have enough to eat, she made him promise never to hunt again. Then she took the bullet out of his arm and packed the wound with a salve she had made.

He kept coming back to see her, first for her doctoring, then for her company. When he married her and moved her into the big house in Wilder where we still live, a lot of people said she had cast a spell on him to make him love her. But Granny always says, "If you take a bullet out of a man, you don't need a potion to make him love you."

Even though he promised Granny he wouldn't hunt, Grandpa sneaked off on a hunting trip one weekend when Granny was pregnant with my mom. A stray bullet from one of his buddies' gun hit him and killed him.

People in Wilder said that Granny had put a death spell on him so she could inherit his money.

"That's just foolishness," Granny always says. "But I did tell that man never to go huntin' again. I seen what would happen to him if he did."

So my mom was raised by just her mother, like Granny had been before her. But Mom grew up in the big house in town instead of a shack in the county, and while she learned about herbs and potions and fortune telling from Granny, she also learned reading, spelling, and math at the Wilder public schools. Mom grew up with one foot in Granny's world and one foot in the world of regular people, which is probably why she spent so much time trying to figure out a logical reason why she can see into other people's minds and futures.

Mom met Dad when she was going to Berea College. He had a ponytail and rode a motorcycle, and they got married right after graduation and moved to Lexington so Dad could go to graduate school. They had been married a little over a year when Mom found out she was pregnant with me.

Now here's the weird part. When Mom was five months pregnant, Dad died in a motorcycle wreck. Mom had begged him not to ride that day.

After Dad died, Mom says she just fell apart. She quit her job in Lexington and moved back to the big house in Wilder. Granny nursed her through her pregnancy and her grief. Granny even delivered me into the world, in the big four-poster bed that's still in the master bedroom.

After some time passed and I was big enough to walk, Mom took a job as a social worker in Morgan, the next town up the road, and Granny took care of me during the day until I was big enough to go to school.

You can imagine the things people say about Granny and Mom. That they're witches. That they killed their husbands as soon as they were pregnant like black widow spiders kill their mates. And since kids hear their parents talking that way about my family, they've never been that anxious to buddy up to me at school.

I get called all kinds of names. The witch girl. The creepy girl. The spooky girl. But they call me that when they're talking to each other. Or they think it, and I hear their thoughts. They don't call me anything to my face. They're too scared of me.

Not that they have a reason to be. I'm different, not dangerous. But to some people's way of thinking, "different" and "dangerous" mean the same thing.

I never try to explain the Sight to kids at school because they'd never understand it. And it is kind of hard to explain. The best I can do is to say that sometimes when I look at a person, I can feel myself entering that person's mind.

The inside of a person's mind is like a movie theatre. It's dark, but then there are these pictures you can see on a big screen. I can hear the words that go along with these pictures, too, just the same as I would if the person was saying them out loud to me.

Like once, I heard Brittany Silcox, who's the most popular girl in the school, thinking about her supposed best friend Caitlin: "The only reason I let her be my best friend is because she's so ugly she makes me look good." Another time when a teacher was handing me back some homework, I heard her think, "This isn't as good as Miranda's work usually is, but as creepy as she and her family are, I'm afraid to give her a bad grade."

One time Mom said, "So many people spend their lives worrying about what other people might be thinking. If they only knew how much harder life is if you actually do know what other people are thinking."

Mom is right. Some days when I'm at school, surrounded by people, my gift throws too much information at me, filling my head with stuff I don't even want to know. Sometimes when classes change and the hall is full of kids, I'm almost deafened by the sound of all their thoughts.

And so, to protect myself, I've always tried to keep my distance from other kids. And other kids have thought they were protecting themselves by keeping their distance from me.

Because of all this distance-keeping, I've managed to make it all the way to middle school without having made a regular friend my age. There's Abigail, of course. But she's not what you'd call a regular friend. She's been dead for over a hundred years.

Chapter Two

I'm lying in my canopy bed, wide awake and dreading school tomorrow. I jump when I hear the knock on the inside of my closet door.

"Come in," I call, barely above a whisper, but the knocking doesn't stop. "You're going to wake up Granny," I hiss, kicking off my covers and jumping out of bed to open the closet door.

"Trick or treat!" Abigail yells, doubling over giggling. Like always she's wearing a powder-blue, drop-waisted dress and high-button shoes. Her blonde ringlets are tied back with a ribbon that matches her dress. "I thought I would make sure you had one trick-or-treater this year," she says.

I grab her by the wrist. She feels solid, but very cold, like somebody who's been playing in the snow for a long time. "Get in here," I laugh, pulling her out of my closet and into my room.

"Do you like my costume?" Abigail twirls in front of me so that her skirt flares. "I'm a ghost this year." She flops down on the red bean bag chair in the corner, but her ringlets and high-button shoes just don't go with a bean bag chair somehow. "Of course, I've been a ghost every year since eighteen ninety-eight, so it's growing rather predictable."

When Abigail was alive, this house was her family's house, and her room was my room. But there were a lot more serious illnesses in the 1800s than there are now, and when Abigail caught scarlet fever at the age of twelve, she ended up passing on to the other side. Her parents, who caught the illness from her, joined her there soon after.

For some reason she's not sure of, though, Abigail can slip between worlds. So while she lives with her parents on the other side, she comes to visit me a few times a week. Partly she does it because she likes being in her old room, but she also does it because she likes me.

Mom can't see Abigail anymore, and Granny has never seen her, but they both know she hangs out in my room pretty often. My room was Mom's room when she was a little girl, and Abigail used to visit her, too. Mom stopped seeing Abigail when she was fourteen years old.

Granny says that when she was a kid, she also had a friend from the other side, a little Indian boy who taught her a lot about using plants and herbs as medicines. But Granny stopped seeing him when she turned fifteen. "Once you start coming into your womanhood, you won't be able to see Abigail no more," Granny told me once. "When you get old enough to give life, you can't see past the world of the living."

It's sad. Abigail is the only friend I've ever had, and it won't be long until I lose her forever.

"Would you like to have a tea party?" Abigail has picked up the teapot from my little china tea set.

I keep the tea set just for decoration, but Abigail is really into pretend tea parties. I guess it's what girls in her time did for fun. "Yeah, okay." I sit down across from her, pick up a tiny tea cup, and let her "pour."

"Did you ask your mother and granny about getting a television for your birthday?" Abigail asks.

"I asked, but they said no. Mom thinks TV kills your imagination and rots your brain. And Granny...well, she's so old-fashioned she won't even cook on an electric stove."

"I wish you could get a TV for your room," Abigail sighs. "I'd love to see it. You tell me about all these marvelous things in the modern world, but I never get to see any of them because your family still lives as though it's the eighteen hundreds."

"Tell me about it." Abigail's right. The only modern convenience we have in our house is a toaster. Other kids have cell phones, but we don't even have a regular telephone. Granny doesn't believe in them. Mom does have a car, a beat-up Toyota she bought the year she graduated from college. It's an awful-looking thing, but Abigail will look at it through the window and ooh and aah at it like it's a brand-new Mercedes.

"I wish Mom could take us on a car ride," I tell Abigail. "We could go to Morgan to the movie theater. And maybe we'd go to Wal-Mart, just so you could see all the kinds of stuff you could buy now."

"I wish we could do that, too." Abigail's voice is soft and dreamy. She knows as well as I do that our little car-trip fantasy will never come true because when Abigail visits, she can't go beyond the walls of my room. She's tried to walk out the door of my room more than once, and every time, it's like there's an invisible wall in my doorway that she can't get past.

"And I wish you could take me to see where you live," I

say. I'm always awfully curious about the other world, but Abigail says it's impossible to explain it in a way I would understand.

"I know," Abigail says. "But there are no visitors there. Only permanent residents." She sets down her cup of pretend tea. "Can we listen to the radio?"

Abigail loves it when we can tune in the Top 40 radio station out of Lexington and dance to pop songs. Lexington's pretty far away, though, so we can't always get the signal. The local stations are all country or gospel.

"We'd better not." I glance at the clock. 11:06. "It's a school night. I should at least try to sleep."

"Can I stay with you? Just until you fall asleep?"

"Okay."

Abigail crawls into bed beside me, and I roll myself up in a quilt so she won't make me too cold. It's nice to have a friend nearby, even a long-dead one, and soon my eyes are closing. When I open them again, the early morning sky is gray, and Abigail is gone.

I drag into home room with a familiar feeling of dread. Caitlin and Britney are in the front row, and Caitlin nudges Britney as I walk past. "Where do you think she gets those clothes?" Caitlin whispers. Britney giggles.

Britney and Caitlin must get their clothes at the same store because they always wear the same thing: name-brand jeans, name-brand tennis shoes, and t-shirts with brand-name slogans on them.

Since Mom and Granny sew my clothes, I don't have a name-brand to my name. Instead I wear long, flowing skirts made out of fabric with pretty patterns'wildflowers, paisley, moons and stars and simple, solid-colored cotton blouses. I wear sandals in the summer and boots and tights in the winter. I don't own a pair of jeans, and the only time I wear tennis shoes is in gym class.

I ignore Britney and Caitlin and take my seat in the back of the room, wishing I had the power to make myself invisible. Mr. Wilkins, who coaches the middle school football team and kinda, sorta teaches sixth grade science, is our home room teacher. I say "kinda, sorta teaches sixth grade science" because all he ever does in class is tell us to read the chapter and answer the questions at the end.

I've seen into his mind a few times. Football is all he thinks about.

"Listen up, team," Mr. Wilkins says, tugging on his gray coach's shorts. "We've got a new student in here. You in the back," he yells like he's shouting across a football field, "stand up and tell us your name."

Every head turns to face the new kid, who's hidden himself in the back left corner, but is now standing up because Mr. Wilkins has given him no choice.

The first thing I notice about him is probably the first thing everybody else notices: he's Asian. In most places, this would be no big deal. But there are no other Asian kids at Wilder Middle. No black kids or Hispanic kids either.

Southeastern Kentucky is a pretty white part of the world, anyway, but Wilder's especially bad. The whole town is as white as the inside of a mayonnaise jar.

The new kid looks down at his desk to keep from looking up at the rest of the class. He has longer hair than the other boys in the class do, and he's wearing baggy olive green pants and a loose-fitting black shirt decorated with orange flames. Everything about him says city kid. I look at his hands, which he's nervously drumming on the desk, and see that he bites his nails.

And just like that whoosh! I'm in his head, racing

through his thoughts, feelings, memories. I see a tall red brick apartment building in a city. There's a basketball court, and he's playing ball with a couple of boys around his age.

Another picture fills the screen: a petite Asian woman, around my mother's age, cooking a food I don't recognize in a tiny kitchen, while an Asian man, whom this kid looks a lot like, sits at the table, reading a huge book and jotting down notes.

Another picture: a moving van driving away from the red brick apartment building, the friends from the basketball court waving goodbye.

Another picture: a mummy, with a wrinkled face peeking out from tattered bandages, slowly moving forward, arms outstretched.

But that's impossible! I think, and as soon as I do, I'm out of the new kid's head and back into my own. My little trip must have only taken a couple of seconds because the kid is still standing there, trying to get up the courage to introduce himself.

"Uh'" he finally says, "I'm Adam So."

"So?" Cody Taylor, the star of the middle school football team, laughs. "So what?"

Everybody laughs, even Mr. Wilkins.

Adam So sits back down. I don't have to see into his mind to know how embarrassed he is.

I fall into the routine of the day: science, math, language arts. I eat my sack lunch at a table by myself.

"What do you reckon she's eating?" one of the girls in the cafeteria line says about me, so low she thinks I can't hear her.

"I don't know," the other girl whispers back. "What do witches eat, anyway? Frog eyeballs? Bat brains?"

I wad up my bread crusts in my napkin and get up from the table. "Sorry to disappoint you girls," I say. "But it was just egg salad."

Out on the playground Cody Taylor and a couple of his dimwit friends have Adam So backed up against the side of the school building. Cody's doing his best to look menacing, and he's doing a pretty good job of it. But I can see the truth inside his tiny brain: he's scared.

"Where you from anyway, So What?" Cody sneers. "I think my granddaddy might've killed some of your people in the war."

Adam sighs like he's bored instead of afraid. "What war did your granddaddy fight in?"

"Vietnam," Cody says.

"Well, then, he didn't kill any of my people," Adam says, looking down at his bitten fingernails. "I was born in America, but my mom and dad are from Korea. But hey, cheer up. If your great-grandad fought in Korea, he might have killed somebody who was related to me."

I bite my cheek so I won't laugh out loud, which would just make Cody madder.

"Are you makin fun of me?" Cody hisses, and his friends start closing in on Adam.

Adam looks at the five big, tall guys surrounding him. "Well, no, I—"

"'Cause I don't like it when people make fun of me!"

I look around to see if any of the teachers are keeping an eye on what's going on, but there's not a grownup in sight. I walk right up to Cody and his sidekicks, stretch my arms toward the sky, close my eyes and try to chant something that sounds like a spell. Too bad that all that pops into my head is a nursery rhyme, so I chant, "Inky pinky ponky, Daddy had a donkey'"

"Hey!" Cody yelps. "What are you doing?"

I look Cody straight in his beady eyes. "I'm calling a curse down on you and your entire family, to be effective immediately, if you don't stop picking on Adam here."

Cody's beady eyes narrow. "Are you faking?"

I look at him with my most serious face. "Do you want to find out for sure?"

Cody looks at his friends, who are paralyzed with fear. "Okay, come on, guys."

"Whoa," Adam says. "That was cool. Or at least I think it was. What happened there?"

"They think I'm a witch."

Adam raises his eyebrows. "No kidding? Well, are you?"

It's almost a trick question. I'm not a witch, but I'm not a regular girl either. But if I can't even explain this to myself, how do I explain it to somebody I just met. "Not really," I finally say. "But sometimes it comes in handy for them to think I am."

When's school's out and I start walking toward home I hear a voice calling, "Hey! Hey, wait up!" But since nobody ever asks me to wait up I just keep right on walking.

Suddenly, though, Adam is next to me, out of breath from running. "Say, don' t you people know what'wait up' means here in the middle of nowhere? I had to run a mile to catch up with you."

I smile. "Sorry. I didn't know you were talking to me."

"Of course I was talking to you. You're the only person I met today who didn't treat me like I had a contagious disease. And I couldn't very well call your name because you never told me what your name was."

I guess I didn't. "Miranda," I say.

Adam grins. "That beats Witch Girl, which seems to be what most people call you."

"Yep," I laugh. "They call Mom and Granny the witch women, so I guess I can look forward to be calling Witch Woman, too, when I grow up." I keep waiting for Adam to leave my side, but he's not showing any signs of it. "Say... you don't have to keep walking with me. Don't you need to go back and get on the bus or something?"

"Nope. I just live up the street. My mom and dad were all excited for us to live somewhere I could walk to school. I have no clue why."

It pops into my head where Adam must live. All the houses up the street are owned by old people who have lived there forever. All except for a two-story house which is about as old as ours and has been sitting empty for as long as I can remember. "Hey," I say, "did your parents buy the old Jameson place?" But then I remember that Adam won't know that everybody in town calls it the old Jameson place, so I add, "I mean, the house on the corner of Laurel and Oak?"

"Yeah, that's the one. Mom says she's been living in little apartments too long and wants a place with some space. Problem is, the house is practically falling apart. But Mom and Dad have watched so many shows on that Do It Yourself channel that they think they can fix the place up in half an hour."

We walk past the Family Drug Store, Louise's House of Hair, and a couple of the empty storefronts that have been popping up downtown ever since they built the Wal-Mart over in Morgan. "So tell me," Adam says, "does your school always give new kids such an un-warm welcome, or is it just me?"

"It's hard to say. To be honest, I can't remember the last

time we had a new kid in school. People don't really move to Wilder because...well, there's not any reason to."

"We have a reason," Adam says. "Dad got one of those special deals in medical school where your tuition will be free if you'll agree to come work in a rural area for three years after you've finished your degree. And this is the rural area. Lucky me."

When we get to the old Jameson place, men on ladders are covering the faded, used-to-be white paint of the house with a fresh coat of candy pink. "Mom wanted the house to be pink," Adam says. "Like my life here isn't going to be hard enough. Say...you want to come in and hang out for a while? We could play Nintendo or something."

I have no idea what Nintendo is, but I'm happy to have somebody being nice to me. "I'd better not. Mom and Granny will worry if I come home late."

"You could call them."

Here's where I have to stop pretending I have a normal family. "Well, no, I couldn't. We don't have a phone. Granny won't have one in the house."

To my shock, Adam grins like it's no big deal. "Old people are weird, aren't they? When my grandparents from Korea come to visit, they always make me bring them a bucket of water to wash with even though we have a perfectly good shower. Well, maybe you can talk to your mom and come hang out after school tomorrow."

Mom will be so amazed that I've made a real, live friend that she'll have to say yes. "Okay. Tomorrow."

Chapter Three

"You have to take off your shoes before you come in," Adam says as we step onto his front porch. "It's an Asian thing."

I pull off my boots and set them on the little shelf by the front door. "I never wear shoes in my house either. I just didn't know I was being Asian."

When we walk into the living room, all the furniture is draped in white sheets, and Adam's mom, the pretty, black-haired lady I recognize from seeing into his thoughts, is standing barefoot on a stepladder, using a roller to paint the wall a cool mint green.

"Hi, Mom. This is Miranda," Adam says.

She looks down at me from her perch on the ladder and smiles. "Hi, Miranda. Sorry this place is such a mess. Help yourself to snacks in the kitchen."

"Thank you," I manage to stutter. I'm not used to people being friendly to me, so I tend to get shy.

"Come on." Adam leads me into the kitchen, which has been painted sunshine yellow, and opens the fridge.

"Want a Coke?"

"Sure." We never have Cokes at our house just water or goat's milk or apple juice or the weird, murky herb teas that Granny makes. I've only drunk Coke a couple of times in my life.

Adam takes a flat paper bag out of a cabinet and puts it inside an appliance that looks like a cross between an oven and a tv set. Soon there is a buttery smell and the pop-pop-pop of popcorn.

"Hey, is that a microwave?" I ask.

Adam looks at me like I just stepped off a space ship. "Uh...yeah."

"Wow, that's so cool! I've heard of them, but I've never seen one cook anything before."

Adam takes out the bag of popcorn and dumps it into a bowl. "Well, you're sure easy to entertain."

I feel my face flush. "I'm sorry. I know I must seem weird. I guess Mom and Granny are old-fashioned. We don't have a microwave or a TV or anything like that."

Adam grabs a handful of popcorn. "Is it because of your religion? Are you Amish or something?"

"No. We're just...different."

Adam shrugs. "Different's okay. You want to see my room?"

"Sure."

The walls of Adam's room are covered with posters and cardboard cut-outs of Frankenstein, Dracula, and the Wolf Man. An inflatable Frankenstein almost as tall as I am is propped up in one corner. An inflatable skeleton hangs by its wrists from chains on the ceiling. "I like your Halloween decorations," I say.

"They're not Halloween decorations," Adam says. "This is always how my room looks."

I suddenly feel like less of a weirdo. Or maybe Adam just seems like more of one. "Well, that's...interesting."

"I love scary movies, scary books, anything scary." He flops down on a pile of cushions in front of his bookshelf. Looking behind him, I see that lots of the books have words like "shivers" or "shudders" in the titles. "Mom and Dad will let me watch any horror movie I want, as long as it was made before nineteen-seventy. They say the ones made after that are too violent. That's my movie collection over there."

I look through the movie titles. "Dracula," "The Invisible Man," "Frankenstein," "Bride of Frankenstein," "The Mummy." I pull "The Mummy" off the shelf and laugh when the face on the cover is the face of the mummy I saw inside Adam's head. So that's where it came from!

"What's funny?" Adam asks.

"Oh, nothing." I look down at the case that holds the movie. "I was just thinking that I've never held a mummy case before." Of course, that wasn't what I was thinking at all.

Adam laughs. "That's pretty good. Say, wanna play a game?"

At my house, whenever somebody says, "Let's play a game," it usually means a card game like Hearts or gin rummy. The kind of game Adam means is a video game with a little man who sucks up ghosts with a vacuum cleaner. I'm sure Abigail would disapprove.

"So," Adam says, after he pushes the game's "start" button, "do you believe in ghosts?"

I figure he'll think I'm nuts if I say, "Sure, my best friend is a ghost," so I just say, "Uh...do you?"

"Sure," he says, sucking up a ghost on the screen. "I don't see any reason why they can't exist. My dad says there's no scientific proof that ghosts exist, but I don't think there's any scientific proof that they don't exist either. Besides, scientists don't know everything."

"I believe in them, too," I say. "There's a lot of stuff in the world that people can't explain."

"Yeah," Adam says. "Ghosts, crop circles, alien abductions, ESP'"

I don't even think before I say, "I have it."

Adam drops the video game controller. "What did you say?"

"I have it. ESP, or something like it. All the women in my family do."

Adam's mouth is open wide. "No way!"

It feels so good to be able to talk about this that my words spill out on top of each other. "We're not witches like people say, but we have something my granny calls the Sight. We can see into people's minds. Like when you stood up in home room yesterday I saw that you used to live in a big red brick apartment building in a city. There was a basketball court and two kids one white and one black that you used to play with."

It's a second or two before Adam can say anything. Then he says, "But you can't know that!"

"Sure I can. I can't explain why I know it, but I know it."

"Can...can you see people's futures, too?"

"Not like Granny can. The Sight gets stronger as you get older, so Mom and Granny have it more than I do. Mostly I can just see people's thoughts, and I can only do that some of the time.

Sometimes I'll get a feeling about somebody's future,

unless it's my own. Mom and Granny and I have the Sight when it comes to other people, but we can't see anything about ourselves."

"Whoa," Adam says, looking at me like I'm an exotic animal at the zoo. "Just...whoa."

"You don't think I'm crazy? Or scary?"

"No way." Adam's face breaks into a big grin. "I think you're the coolest girl I've ever met. When can I meet your mom and granny?"

When I get home, Mom and Granny are both in the front yard. Mom is raking leaves, and Granny is standing over a huge iron pot that has a fire under it. Whatever she's stirring stinks to high heaven.

Granny claims she doesn't understand why everybody thinks she's a witch, and then she does stuff like stand out in the yard wearing a long black dress and stirring a giant pot of what might as well be witch's brew.

"Your granny took a notion to make some lye soap today," Mom says, pushing more leaves into a pile. She's still in her work clothes'a long, peacock-blue fringed skirt with a matching fringed vest. Her bracelets jangle as she rakes.

The smell makes my eyes water. "Ugh! I don't see how you can stand to smell that stuff, Granny, let alone use it on your skin. I'll take a bar of Ivory any day."

"Store-bought soap don't get you clean like lye soap," Granny says, pushing back a steel-gray braid to keep it from falling in the pot.

"Yep, lye soap cleans the skin right off your body," Mom says, smiling. She looks at me. "So your visit with your friend was good?"

She knows it was good by looking at me. She's just asking to be polite. "Yeah. He wants to come over sometime. Is that okay?"

"Your friends are always welcome here," Mom says.

I laugh. "My friends? I only have one friend. Well, one living friend."

"Well, it's better to have one real friend than a hundred false ones, like some people have," Mom says. "Hold this bag for me, will you?"

I hold the leaf bag while Mom fills it. "The thing is," I say, "his parents want to meet y'all. They don't like Adam to go over to somebody's house until they've met their family."

"Well," Mom says, stuffing more leaves in the bag, "maybe we should have them over for dessert and coffee or something."

Granny looks up from her stirring with a strange gleam in her eye. "I never met no people from the Orient before. I'd like to ask them some questions about herbs and healing... and ancient mysteries."

This is exactly the kind of thing I was afraid Granny would say. "Um, Granny," I start, "you can ask Adam about those kind of things when he's here by himself, but when his parents come to meet you, maybe it would be a good idea for you not to be so...spooky."

Granny looks up from her steaming cauldron. Her one-eyed cat rubs against the hem of her long black dress. "How am I spooky?" she says.

Chapter Four

Adam and his parents will be here in an hour. Mom and Granny are washing up the supper dishes, and I've been given the job of feeding the goats and chickens before our company gets here. I'm grateful to have a job that gets me out of the house for a few minutes because I'm a nervous wreck.

I can't get the picture out of my mind of Adam's parents, horrified and dragging him out of the house, probably while holding up a crucifix in front of us. I don't know if this picture is me seeing the future, or just me being nervous.

I have to hand it to Mom, though. She's really thrown herself into making a good impression. She made a pie from the blackberries we picked and froze this summer, and she put on a pretty purple batik dress and silver dangly earrings. Granny is in her same black dress and black stockings and silver braids. But it's not like I expected her to put on a flowered dress and apron like a grandma in a picture book.

The two goats see me coming and stand up on their hind legs with their front hooves propped on the fence. "Hey, Naomi. Hey, Ruth," I say. Granny names all of her animals out of the Bible. Ruth and Naomi are Tennessee Fainting Goats. They're beautiful white goats with golden eyes, and true to their name, they will faint dead away if they're startled. When I was a little kid, I got into a lot of trouble for banging on pots and pans to make the goats faint.

The goats don't seem to hold my pranks against me, though. When I enter their pen, they butt me lovingly, and while I fill their feed buckets, they bleat in appreciation.

I go to the chicken coop next. There are five hens (Mary Magdalene, Esther, Rachel, Sarah, and Delilah) and one rooster named Samson. The hen's job is to lay eggs, and Samson's job is to strut around and show off his good looks. I scatter feed on the ground, and they peck happily.

I still have forty-five minutes to go until Adam and his parents get here. I go back to the house, climb the stairs to my room, and try to read a mystery. But I can't concentrate. When the doorbell finally does ring, I jump about a foot, just like it wasn't the sound I was expecting all along.

You can tell we don't get much company because when I go downstairs, Mom and Granny are standing in front of the door, arguing about who should answer it.

"Maybe Miranda should answer it," Mom says. "Adam is her friend."

"No," Granny says. "It ain't proper to let a child answer the door. The door should be answered by the lady of the house."

"Well, then, who's the lady of the house? You or me?" Mom sounds exasperated.

"Well," Granny ways, "some folks would say it's me on account of,'"

I can tell Granny's about to go into a lengthy speech while the Sos are waiting outside and wondering if anybody's home. Proper or not, I open the door myself.

Adam is standing in the doorway between his mom and dad, who have dressed up for the occasion. Mrs. So is wearing a simple blue dress in almost the same shade as her husband's tie. I look into Adam's mind and see that he's nervous, too, not nervous about our house being spooky or my family being weird, but nervous that his family, even though he loves them, will do something that will embarrass him. His thoughts are the same as mine, and I instantly feel better.

"Hi," I say. "Dr. and Mrs. So, this is my mom, Sarah Jasper, and my granny, Irene Chandler."

"Oh!" my mom says, startled out of her argument with Granny. "How nice to meet you. Come in."

The Sos come in, but first they leave their shoes in a neat little row on the front porch.

I keep waiting for Granny to say something, but she just stares at the Sos without even blinking.

"I thought we'd have dessert in the living room," Mom says. "Why don't you all sit down? Miranda, come and help me in the kitchen for a minute."

Dr. and Mrs. So settle on the wine-colored camel back sofa. Adam sits in the green wing-backed chair. All the furniture in the living room is heavy and dark and old and looks like it's been here ever since the house was built. Old photos of the women in my family hang on the walls, women with high collars and their hair in buns staring with eyes that look like they can see right into your soul. And if these women were still alive, they could do just that.

Methuselah, Granny's African gray parrot, stirs in his cage and squawks, "a whistling gal and a crowing hen always come to a bad end."

"Oh!" Mrs. So laughs, sounding startled. "The bird talks."

"All the time," Mom says. "He's practically an encyclopedia of old sayings."

"My ma taught him how to talk. He belonged to her until she died," Granny says. "he's just about as old as I am." Granny gets up and opens the cage, and Methuselah hops on her shoulder, pirate-style. Mr. and Mrs. So look fascinated, but it's the same kind of fascination that comes from seeing a two-headed cow or something else too weird to be explained.

Adam is all smiles. We haven't disappointed him. My family beats a horror movie any day.

Methuselah nuzzles his beak in Granny's braids. "Be friendly. Talk to the folks, honey," Granny says.

Methuselah squawks, "There's more than one way to choke a dog with butter."

As Mom and I head toward the kitchen, I whisper, "Are you sure it's a good idea to leave her alone with them?"

"Mercy, Miranda, you sound as bad as half the people in this town." Mom sets a pot of coffee on a tray loaded with cups and saucers, cream and sugar, and glasses of milk for Adam and me.

"What do you think she'll do? Cast a spell on them?"

"No." I pick up the tray that holds the blackberry pie, forks, and dessert plates. "Just scare them off."

"Don't be silly," Mom says, picking up the coffee tray. "Dr. and Mrs. So are sophisticated. I'm sure he's had to deal with all kinds of people as patients, and believe it or not, there are people in the world who are weirder than your granny."

When we go back into the living room, Granny still has

Methuselah perched on her shoulder and is saying, "Over in your part of the world, they say sang has mighty strong healing powers. I ain't never had much luck with it myself, though. How do you use it?"

"I'm afraid I've never heard of anything called sang," Dr. So says.

"She means ginseng," Mom says as she cuts the pie. "Sang is just what mountain people call it."

"Ah, yes," Dr. So says. "I have heard of it, then. But I'm afraid I don't know much about folk remedies, Mrs. Chandler. My background is in Western medicine." His smile is open and friendly, like Adam's.

"Well, I could teach you about the old mountain ways of healing, if you ever took a notion to learn," Granny says. "I know what kind of herbs to mix for different kinds of complaints and what words from the Bible you say to clear up a boil or a sty."

"Dr. and Mrs. So, where were you living before you moved to Wilder?" Mom interrupts Granny, and I'm glad. "Boston," Mrs. So says.

"Oh, I've always wanted to take Miranda there and show her all the historical sites," Mom says, offering around cream and sugar.

"You ought to take her to Salem," Adam says, "to the witch museum."

Mrs. So giggles. It's a nice, bubbly sound. "Oh, the witch museum! What a tourist trap! We took Adam there because we thought it would teach him about the Salem witch trials, about how people can be persecuted because they're different."

Dr. So laughs. "But all the trip to the witch museum did was get Adam obsessed with the idea that witchcraft and witches might really exist. It was all just another horror movie to him."

"I knowed a woman back in the hills that they said was a witch," Granny says. "They said she turned her neighbor's cow's milk into pure blood. Of course, lots of folks said my ma was a witch, too."

"Mom, can I show Adam my room?" I blurt. I feel my mind starting to seek out what's going on in Dr. and Mrs. So's minds, to find out what's behind the polite expressions on their faces, even though I don't want to know.

"Sure, honey, if it's okay with his parents."

Dr. and Mrs. So nod, and I lead Adam up the stairs.

"Your grandma should have been in some of those old horror movies," Adam says once we're out of earshot. "She would've been great as the old gypsy that tells the guy he's going to turn into a werewolf."

"I hope she's not freaking out your parents too bad."

"No, Dad thinks she's interesting, I can tell. And your mom seems really nice."

"Yeah, Granny's nice, too. She just takes some getting used to." I lead him down the hall, past some embarrassing baby pictures of me. "So...this is my room."

Adam takes it all in, the antique canopy bed, the purple and gold paisley wallpaper, the lamps I drape with scarves because Abigail can't handle bright light.

"I like it," he declares. "The cool thing about all these old houses is the weird angles of the walls." He cocks his head to take in the way the walls bend and turn. "Like this one's slanted over here, and this one sticks out all funny. It's so different from the room I had in my old apartment, which was like a shoebox, only smaller."

"Mom says this room was hell to wallpaper."

"I guess so. It's a lot like my room in my house, really. I

guess the only thing I like about Wilder is my room." He looks at me. "And I like you, too. As a friend, I mean."

I feel embarrassed and happy at the same time. "Thanks," I say. "Well, I don't have a Nintendo or a TV, but,"

Knock, knock, knock. The sound is coming from inside my closet door. What am I supposed to say' *But I do have a ghost?*

I look at Adam's face. He's definitely freaking out. "Okay, Adam," I say. "I've got something to show you, well, not some thing, really. And chances are you won't be able to see anything at all. But you're perfectly safe, so don't be scared, okay?"

Adam swallows hard, but says, "O-okay."

I open the closet door, and in flounces Abigail. "Oh, you didn't tell me your new friend was from the Orient!" She claps her hands. "How exotic!"

Adam looks like someone who wants to run but whose feet have been Superglued to the floor. "Uh...Miranda, where's that voice coming from?"

"You can hear her?"

Adam nods.

"Can you see anything?"

He looks where Abigail is standing. "I see a gray mist, like the steam that rises from a tea kettle."

Abigail laughs. "Well, I'm not much to look at from your point of view, am I? Miranda, tell him what I really look like."

"Adam," I say. "This is Abigail. She has long blonde hair and blue eyes and is very pretty. She's wearing an old-fashioned light blue dress with a big bow around the waist."

"The same dress I was buried in," Abigail says, looking down at it in disgust. "And I am sick of it, let me tell you.

But the clothes you're buried in are the clothes you're stuck with for all eternity. When you're on this side, that is. On the other side we don't need clothes. We don't have bodies...exactly."

"So," Adam manages to get out, "you're a ghost?"

"Well, I prefer being called a spirit, but you may use the G- word if you feel strongly about it."

Adam looks in Abigail's direction, then looks at me. "Whoa. Miranda, when I asked you the other day if you believed in ghosts, I didn't think you were going to open your closet door and one would come walking out."

I let myself feel what he feels. It's shock, but it's a happy kind of shock, like a little kid who's walked into the living room on Christmas Eve night and seen Santa Claus.

"Surprise," I say, grinning at him. But then a thought crosses my mind. "Abigail, you always said the reason you can appear to me is because I have the Sight. Does this mean that Adam has the Sight, too?"

Abigail sits on the edge of my dresser and fiddles with a cat figurine. "No. If he had the Sight, he could see me in the flesh, like you do. Adam can hear me and see vapors where I am because his mind is more open than most people's. He doesn't close his mind off to things that are...extraordinary." She shifts the figurine from hand to hand. "Do you think I'm extraordinary, Adam?"

"Yes," Adam says, his eyes on the figurine that Amanda is holding. To his eyes, it must look like it's floating in space.

"I think you're extraordinary, too," Abigail says. "Most people would have run out of here as soon as I appeared, or at least would have accused Miranda of playing a joke on them." She sets down the figurine and looks right at Adam. "But you took me at face value. And I can tell you're very cultured. Not like most people in this town. Where are you from in the Orient?"

"I'm American. From Boston."

"Oh, Boston!" Abigail smiles. "I went there when I was alive! I came from up East, to...Philadelphia. But then Papa decided to open a store in this dreadful little town, and I caught scarlet fever and died. But enough about me... tell me about yourself, Adam. I haven't talked to a living person other than Miranda since...well, since Miranda's mother was a girl."

"Well..." Adam sputters. "I'm kind of a...student of the supernatural."

Abigail laughs. "Are you? Well, Miranda and I would make excellent teachers. Wouldn't we, Miranda?"

"I guess we would." All of a sudden I feel as happy as I can ever remember feeling, probably because for the first time I have two real friends.

"Well, you know," Adam says, "there is something I'd like to ask both of you'"

"Adam!" Mrs. So's voice calls up the stairs. "Your dad's pager just went off. We have to go."

Disappointment and something else worry? show on Adam's face. He says, "Well, I guess I'll have to ask you another time." But even as he says it, I am seeing into his thoughts: I have to tell somebody who can help me understand what's going on, because if I wait too long it might be too late.

Chapter Five

Adam is sitting across from me in the school cafeteria, dragging a droopy french fry through a puddle of ketchup. He lifts the fry like he's going to eat it, then lets it fall back on his plate.

"So why don't you tell me what you were going to ask me?" I say, wadding up my paper lunch sack. "If you don't, I'll just dig around in your brain till I find out what it is."

"I'll tell you later." Adam glances around the crowded cafeteria. "In private."

"We might as well be in private right now. Look around. Who's paying attention to us?" The popular girls are all sitting at one table, and the popular boys are all sitting at another. The poor kids and the kids from way out in the country take up the rest of the tables. Adam and I are sitting at the only "table for two" in the cafeteria.

"Well," Adam whispers, leaning over the table, "you remember the first time you came over to my house when I asked you if you believed in ghosts?"

"Yeah."

"Well, there was a reason I was asking." Adam looks around the room, then whispers even more softly, "Ever since we moved into this house, weird things have been happening."

"What kind of weird things?"

"Well," Adam says, "you remember when you came over and Mom was painting the living room wall?"

"Yeah."

"Well, that was the third time she painted it."

"So? She didn't like the color once she got it on the wall. My mom's like that, too."

"No," Adam says in a regular voice, then looks around to make sure nobody's listening. "It's more than that. See, when we first moved in, there was this raggedy old wallpaper in the living room. Blue flowers on a white background that had turned yellow with age. But there was this one place on the wallpaper with two black hand prints on it. The hand prints were smeared, like a person with dirty hands smacked the wall and then slid his hands down it all the way to the floor."

"So? That's not that weird," I say.

"Wait. I've not gotten to the weird part. Mom rented a steamer thing and steamed off all the old wallpaper so she could paint the wall. She painted it eggshell white the first time, and as soon as the paint dried, those hand prints came back, right in the same spot."

"Okay," I say. "That's weird."

"It gets weirder. Now Mom and Dad aren't superstitious. To them, science and logic can explain anything. So Mom figured maybe the hand prints were some kind of deep stain she just hadn't noticed before. So she painted over them, a shade darker this time. They came back. Then she tried the mint green. And they came back again. I heard her tell Dad that she guessed the only way to cover the hand prints was to paint the living room wall black to match them. Then there's the bathroom thing."

The bell rings, which means we have to stand in line with a bunch of other people to throw away our leftovers. "What bathroom thing?" I say, wondering if I even want to know.

"Hey, look," Cody Taylor hollers. "Old So What is in love with the Witch Girl."

"Just ignore him," Adam whispers, but instead I look straight at Cody. I take the moon-shaped silver pendant I'm wearing around my neck, lift it up to my lips, and kiss it. Then I point my index finger at Cody, who takes two steps backward and bumps into one of his dumb friends.

"Wow," Adam says as we walk away, "what did that mean?"

"Not a thing," I say, "but he'll think it means something."

After school, I stop by Adam's house. The living room walls are still mint green, but there's no sign of the hand prints. "I don't see anything."

"They're still here." Adam points toward an end table with a tall lamp on it. "Mom just moved that against the wall to hide them."

We scoot back the table, and there they are, a little below midway down the wall, two black hand prints, fingers spread apart, then hand-sized smears all the way down to the baseboard. "They're smaller than I thought they'd be," I say. "Like a woman's hand prints, or maybe an older kid's."

I spread out my fingers and place my hands on the prints on the wall. The second I make contact, pain pounds through me, a heavy, thudding pain in the back of my head. And fear. Fear spreads through me until it is even stronger than the pain. But fear of what? Fear of dying from whatever is causing the pain? No, there's more to it than that'a feeling that if I die now, it'll be much better than what I have to face if I live.

"Miranda! Are you okay?" Adam is leaning over me. To my surprise, I'm lying flat on my back on his living room floor.

"Uh...yeah." The pain is gone, except for a dull ache in the back of my head.

"You fell backwards," Adam says. "Actually, it looked more like you were pushed backwards. I tried to catch you, but it happened too fast."

"Is everything all right?" Mrs. So has rushed in, no doubt having heard the thunk my head made when it hit the floor.

I force myself to sit up. "Yes, ma'am. I just tripped on a lamp cord."

Mrs. So looks at the lamp cord, which is pretty far away from where I am, and then at me, with the expression of a mother who's wondering if she should let her kid hang out with such a strange person. "Okay...well, there are snacks in the kitchen if you want them."

"Thanks," Adam and I both say.

When Mrs. So is gone I say, "So let me see your bathroom."

"After what just happened, I think you may have seen enough for one day."

"No, really. Let me see it."

Adam sighs. "Okay." He leads me upstairs to the room next door to his. Like the bathroom in our house, it's old-fashioned but has been updated. The big, claw-footed tub has had a shower added onto it, and a new lighted mirror hangs over the old-fashioned sink.

"It won't work unless you close the door," Adam says.

I have no clue what he's talking about, but I close the door anyway. Adam leans over the bathtub and turns on the shower full blast. "It'll take a minute," he says.

I, of course, have no idea what he means, but I wait anyway. Soon steam from the shower is filling the room, making everything hot and misty. Adam's glasses are fogged up.

"There it is!" he says. "The mirror! Look at the mirror!"

I turn around and see it. The mirror is completely fogged over, like Adam's glasses, except for one short line of cursive writing that looks like it's been drawn on the glass with someone's fingertip. I step closer and read the words: *He is innocent.*

I touch the mirror, wondering if I can get some kind of feeling from it, like I did with the hand prints, but all I feel is wet glass. "Does it say this every time?"

"Yep," Adam says. "It's always '*He is innocent.*' At first, I thought it might just be regular writing that hadn't gotten cleaned off good. But check this out."

He opens the towel closet and takes out a bottle of spray cleaner and a washcloth. He sprays over the words and wipes them off. Within seconds, as soon has the steam has fogged the mirror back up, the words are back again.

"Do your parents know about this?" I ask.

"No. They shower in the other bathroom. And I haven't told them about it. I know the hand print thing freaks them out even though they pretend it doesn't. I don't want to give them something else to pretend not to be freaked out about."

I look at the words one more time. "Well, if we don't get out of here, your mom's going to freak out anyway... about why we're spending so much time together in the bathroom."

Adam grins. "Good point." He opens the bathroom door. "You want to play some Nintendo?"

"No, I have to head home," I say. "But this has certainly been...interesting. If Abigail pops by tonight, I'll tell her about it and see what she has to say."

"Miranda," Adam looks at me, and I feel a surge of fear shoot from him. "Do you think I should be...scared?"

"No," I say. "The person who left those hand prints was afraid, but I don't think what they were afraid of is still in this house. And the words on the mirror aren't threatening or anything. They seem like..information. Like something somebody wants you to know."

"But what do they want me to know? You're psychic; you're supposed to know this stuff."

"I'm psychic about living people, not haunted bathroom mirrors. I have no idea what the presence in this house is trying to tell you. But I'd sure like to find out."

Chapter Six

"Oh, you didn't tell me your friend lived in the Jameson place." Abigail is flipping through an issue of *Seventeen* magazine I picked up for her. "Look at this," she says, pointing to a model in a tummy-baring top and low-rider jeans. "In my day, girls weren't even supposed to show their ankles."

"What do you know about the Jameson place?" I ask, trying to keep her on the subject, even though she seems to find the magazine a lot more interesting than my talk of ghostly hand prints and haunted bathroom mirrors.

"I don't know much, really." Abigail waves a perfume sample under her nose and sighs, "I wish I could smell." She sets down the magazine. "I can remember people in this house talking about the murders, but I don't know any details. When they happened, I had been dead for years."

"The murders?"

"Yes, the murders. In the Jameson house...sometime in

the nineteen-thirties, I suppose. But you know me...all the dates after my death are hazy. Your grandmother should remember them, though. She would have been a schoolgirl when they happened." Abigail looks faraway for a second, then mutters, "Helen and Mildred."

"Helen and Mildred?" I say.

"The Jameson sisters. The ones who were murdered. I used to play with them when they were girls."

I scoot to the edge of my bed. "Really? What were they like?"

Abigail thinks for a second, then says, "I liked Helen. She was quiet and shy but nice. Mildred, though, was different. 'Mil-dread,' I used to call her. She was always telling her sister what to do in the rudest possible way. She changed the rules of games so she would win. If she was playing in here, she would even rearrange the things in my room so they would suit her better."

My arms prickle with goose bumps at the thought of the murdered Jameson sisters having played in this room years ago. "They came to this house?"

"Yes," Abigail says. "A few times. Their parents and my parents knew each other socially. I think I might have enjoyed playing alone with Helen, but Helen never came without Mildred. They were a matched set, like salt and pepper shakers. I could never figure out why Helen let Mildred tell her what to do since Mildred was two years younger than she was. It was just their personalities, I suppose. I guess there have always been bossy kids and kids who let themselves be bossed around,"

I say. "So do you think it could be the Jameson sisters leaving messages on the bathroom mirror?"

"It probably is. Often, when one meets an untimely end, through violence or an accident or an early illness, one feels a strong need to communicate with the world of the living." Abigail's lips turn up in a half-smile. "I speak from experience, of course."

"Yeah," I say, "but you do speak...out loud so I can hear you. And Adam, too, even if he can't see you. If the spirits of the Jameson sisters want to communicate so much, why don't they just to talk to Adam? If he can hear you, he can hear them."

"Not necessarily," Abigail says, walking over to look at herself in the dresser mirror. "Not all spirits are as able to communicate with the living as I am. There are different categories of spirits who can communicate with the living on different levels. There are the signers, for example. They cannot speak or be seen but can leave messages like the hand prints on your friend's wall, or, on good days, the writing on his mirror." Abigail braids her hair as she looks at herself. As soon as she lets go of the braid, her hair goes back to the way it was before, in the same ringlets she was wearing when they buried her.

"And then there are the spirits like me," she says. "The talkers, who can appear and talk to a few chosen people." She piles her hair on top of her head. "And then there are the rappers."

I can't get a picture of a ghost wearing baggy pants and saying "yo" out of my mind. "You mean...like rap music?"

Abigail looks at me blankly, letting her hair return to ringlets. "No. They rap'" she knocks her fist on the dresser'" like this. They can't speak, but they try to communicate by banging on things. You should ask Adam if he's heard any unusual noises. Sometimes signers can be rappers as well."

She flops back down in the beanbag chair and picks up the magazine. "Ooh, look at this," she says, pointing to a page. "The New Victorian look" She shows me a photo of long-haired girls wearing dresses with puffy sleeves and heavy lace collars. "If I could only get out of this room, I'd be quite fashionable, wouldn't I?"

We get up early at my house. Samson the rooster crows at sunrise, and then it's time to gather the eggs and milk the goats and give all the animals their breakfast. After our chores, Mom and Granny and I always sit down to our own breakfast of fresh eggs, hot biscuits, and cooked apples, with coffee for the grownups and goat's milk for me.

When I told Adam how long I've usually been awake before I come to school, he was shocked. He said he wakes up fifteen minutes before the bell rings and grabs a Pop Tart on his way out the door.

This morning at breakfast, as Granny is sliding a fried egg off a spatula and onto my plate, she says, "Well, mercy, honey, who told you that?"

What Granny's talking about is the question that was in my head but hadn't made it to my mouth yet, namely: *So what do you know about the murder of Helen and Mildred Jameson?*

It's not unusual for Granny to answer a question before you ask it. The longer a woman has the Sight, the stronger it grows, and so Granny's powers are much stronger than mine and quite a bit stronger than Mom's.

Mom's are still strong, though. Sometimes I'll walk into the living room and Mom and Granny will be sitting there, and I'll know that even though they aren't saying anything out loud, they're talking to each other.

"Abigail told me a little about it," I say. "But she didn't know much. She said she used to play with the Jameson girls when she was a kid."

"Your friend Adam lives in the Jameson house, doesn't he?" Mom says, her silver bracelets clanging as she pours goat's milk in her coffee.

"Yeah, and there's been some weird stuff going on... messages on mirrors, hand prints that won't go away." I figure I might as well tell Mom and Granny about it After all, it's not like I can hide the truth from them.

"Restless spirits," Granny says, pouring molasses on a biscuit. "They ort to burn some sage in the house. If the spirits are evil, that might run them off." Methuselah flies over and perches on her shoulder, and she feeds him a bite of biscuit. "Course, if the spirits meant them harm, they probably would've harmed them by now."

"Abigail thinks it might be the spirits of the Jameson sisters trying to communicate with the living," I say.

"Could be," Granny says. She takes a thoughtful slurp of coffee. "It was a terrible thing done in that house."

I'm on the edge of my chair. "Tell me about it."

"Another time, Miranda," Mom says. "This is far too upsetting a subject to discuss at the breakfast table. And besides, you need to get ready for school."

"I am ready, and school doesn't start for another hour. Tell me, Granny."

Mom sighs and takes her breakfast plate to the sink. "How lucky I am to have a daughter who's just as morbid as my mother," she says.

"Well, honey," Granny begins. "All I know is what I got told. I was younger than you are now when it happened. The Jameson sisters was as different as only two sisters can be. Mildred was the bold one, strong-willed and bossy. She gave piano lessons to some of the girls in town, who was scared to death of her. Helen, though, was shy and sweet, wouldn't say boo to a goose, that one. But she loved children and taught at the elementary school. Younguns loved her as much as they feared Mildred."

Granny pushes away her coffee cup. "Everybody respected the Jameson sisters. Their daddy had been a bigwig at the mines before he died, and they were both respectable, churchgoing ladies. So it was a real shock that afternoon when shots rang out at the Jameson place. When the sheriff got there, there was three people lying in the floor. Mildred and Helen had both been shot, and laying a little ways from them near the living room wall was this little colored boy"

"Mother, don't say 'colored,'" Mom says while she's packing my lunch at the kitchen counter. "At the very least say 'black.'"

"Black is the color of mourning," Granny says. "It's the color of clothes I put on every day, and I ain't yet seem a person with skin the same color as this dress. I think 'colored' sounds happier than 'black.' And Sarah, you know as good as I do that it ain't what you call people, it's how you think of 'em that matters. Look in my head right now, and tell me you think I'm prejudiced."

"I never said you were prejudiced," Mom says. "I just meant 'colored' doesn't sound nice."

I look at the clock on the wall. Before long I'll have to leave for school. "Can't you two argue later and tell me about the Jameson murder now?"

"You two talk about what you like. I'm getting ready for work." Mom strides out of the room, her bracelets jangling.

"So there was this little colored boy," Granny says when Mom's gone. "He used to deliver newspapers and do odd jobs for people. His name was Charlie Thomas, but everybody called him Charlie T. And he was there at the scene of the murder, laying on the living room floor. He had been knocked out cold with a fireplace poker. And in his hand was the gun that killed both the Jameson sisters."

"Did he kill them?" By this time I've so totally forgotten about the plate in front of me that I accidentally stick my elbow in my cooked apples.

"Well," Granny says, setting Methuselah down so he can eat off her plate, "this place bein' like it is, and times bein' what they was, everybody thought Charlie T was the murderer. Back then if somebody's skin was dark, that alone was enough reason for most people to think they was guilty of something. But see, there was always things about the whole story that just didn't add up. Like, why would Charlie T want to kill the Jameson ladies? Some folks said it had somethin' to do with them not paying him for the odd jobs he'd been doing. But is a few nickels reason enough to kill two people? And the question that always bothered me is how Charlie T could've managed to shoot Miss Helen straight through the head at the same time she was braining him with a poker."

"I don't guess the sheriff asked any of those questions," I say.

"Nope." Granny scoops up Methuselah and cradles him in her arms like a baby. "He arrested Charlie T then and there. And that night the Klan rode through the colored section of town with shotguns, rounded up all the folks and put them on the first freight train out of town. And that's why there ain't no colored people in Wilder."

My eyes snap shut, but with my inner eyes I can see into the mind of the past. Horses ridden by white-hooded figures gallop through a neighborhood of tarpaper shacks. A huge wooden cross is driven into the ground, then set on fire. The white-hooded men jab the noses of their guns into the ribs of black men, while a little brown baby, his big brown eyes reflecting the flaming cross, cries and clutches at his mother's dress. In line they march, mothers, fathers, and children, shoved at gunpoint to the waiting train. The air burns with hate.

"Miranda! Miranda, come back!"

It's my mother's voice. When I open my eyes, she is leaning over, and I am somehow lying on the kitchen floor. "The hate," I gasp. "The fear."

Mom lifts me so I am resting my head on her lap. "I know, baby. Your Sight is getting stronger, if you can feel people's emotions from so long ago." She strokes my hair, and then I see that Granny is beside me, too.

"I made you some chamomile tea," she says. "It'll settle you." She looks at my mother. "You were right, Sarah. It was too early in the morning to speak of such things."

"No," Mom says, as I sit up and take the teacup. "You were right to talk about it. All these years I've protected Miranda from Wilder's shameful past. But I should have known...the longer you keep a difficult truth a secret, the more it will hurt when the secret comes out."

I hold the teacup in my shaking hands. I can still feel the heat from the burning cross. "I hurt so much. For Charlie T, for all those people."

"I know," Mom says. "Maybe you should stay home from school today and let Granny take care of you."

"No," I say, and as soon as I say it, I feel calm again. "I need to talk to Adam. I need to tell him what the message on his bathroom mirror meant."

"You never did tell us what the writing on the mirror said," Granny says.

I swallow hard. "It says, 'He is innocent.'"

Chapter Seven

In home room before the bell rings, Adam leans over to me and whispers, "But even if Charlie T was innocent, what are we supposed to do about it? The guy's probably dead by now anyway."

"Maybe he is, and maybe he isn't," I say. "But either way, I think what the Jameson sisters want is for us to prove that Charlie didn't do it."

"Why do you think they're calling on a couple of kids to do such a big job?"

"I don't know," I say. "Maybe because most adults won't listen to them, but we will. Besides, it's not that big a job If Charlie T is innocent, all we have to do is find out who's guilty."

"'All we have to do?'" Adam laughs. "You make it sound so easy, solving a murder case that adults couldn't solve when it happened."

"But nobody even tried to solve it. They just assumed

that Charlie T was guilty because he was black. Adam, you know what it's like being different in this town now. Just think about how much worse it must have been seventy years ago. How can you not want to help Charlie T?"

Adam throws his hands up. "Okay, you win, but I don't think we're going to get anywhere with this." He takes a deep breath. "Okay, so what do we do first, Nancy Drew?"

When I grin at him, he grins back. "Research. We need to read everything there is to read about the case."

"Well," Adam says, "why don't you come over to my house after school? We can get online and see what we can find."

"Sure," I say, then I remember something and cringe. "Wait, I can't. I promised Granny I'd go with her to visit her friend in the hospital." Granny loves nothing better than visiting friends in the hospital and smuggling in all kinds of herbs and potions she's mixed up' 'the medicine that'll really make them better,' she says.

Granny always takes me along on these hospital visits because her old eyes have a hard time reading the small print on the signs and doors, and so if she goes alone, she tends to wander around lost, too proud to ask for directions. For somebody with psychic powers, Granny sure can get herself lost in a hurry.

"Hmm..." Adam says, "Well, I could meet you at the hospital, then. I go over there some afternoons and help Dad. He sends me to fetch sodas for patients and read to them if they're too sick to read themselves...maybe make small talk with them. He says sometimes the best medicine for cancer patients is to get their minds off their sickness. I bet after I'm done helping Dad, he'd let us use the computer in his office."

When I get home from school, Granny is at the kitchen table, shoving stalks of some nasty smelling dried herb into a vase of dried flowers. "See," she says, "it looks just like a regular vase of flowers, but these plants here is powerful healers. Daisy can ask the nurse to bring her some hot water for tea, then let them leaves steep in the hot water for a spell. If she drinks that right regular, it'll fix her up better than them old pills the doctor's giving her."

"Yes, ma'am," I say because there's nothing else I can say. There's no point in arguing with Granny.

She puts one last stalk into the vase and says, "There, now. If you'll tote the flowers, I'll get my stick, and we'll be ready to go."

Granny's walking stick is handmade, with a carved snake that coils all the way up it; the stick's handle is the snake's head. She says the snake on the staff is a symbol of healing, but I don't think other people see it that way. Between Granny's snake stick, her head-to-toe black clothing, and the long gray braid trailing down her back, it's no wonder that as we walk down the sidewalk, several people cross the street to keep from passing her.

Outside the Family Dollar Store, a toddler with white-blond hair points at Granny and screams, "Look, Mommy! The witch!"

His mother pulls him close, whispering, "Hush! She'll eat you!"

If Granny notices them, she doesn't let on.

The hospital is on the other side of town, so by the time we get there, I'm pretty sick of carrying Granny's vase of flowers. When we walk through the hospital's clean glass doors, the antiseptic smell hits me first, then the feeling I always get in hospitals: flashes of other people's pain and sickness. Granny gets it, too, so the first time it happened to me, she recognized it. "Just let it wash over you for a minute, then you'll be all right," she said. And I was.

Since I'm not too proud to ask, I let the lady at the front desk give me directions to Granny's friend Daisy's room. As Granny and I walk down the fluorescent lit hall of patients' rooms, Granny says, "Read me the names on the doors. I want to know who's here."

"Granny, that's nosey."

"It ain't nosey if you're a healer and want to know who's sick. I might need to bring somebody else some herbs."

As we walk past the doors, I softly read the names, Bertha Todd, Margie Cox, Harold Buchanan, hoping the people behind the doors can't hear me. The next name I see is Daisy's.

Daisy Perkins is one of the few real friends Granny has in Wilder. She says her late husband's mother had the Sight, so she knows it's not something to be afraid of.

When we go into Daisy's room, she's propped up on the pillows in bed, her white hair flattened to her head. "Well, look who's here!" she says, her wrinkled face breaking into a smile. "My sweet friend and her pretty granddaughter."

"We brought you some flowers," I say, glad to be able to finally set the vase down.

"But they ain't just for looking at," Granny says, touching the leaves. "You'll want to make a tea out of these here. They'll have you on your feet in no time."

"I'm ready to be back on my feet and back in my house," Daisy says. "The doctor says it won't be much longer til I can go home. They think that one little place they cut out was all the cancer I had. I'm so grateful to you, Irene, for telling me to go to the doctor." Daisy looks at me. "Do you know, honey, that your Granny could tell I had the cancer just by squeezing my hand? She saw me in the store one day, squeezed my hand to say hello, then she kindly winced and said, "Daisy, honey, I don't want to scare you none, but you need to go to the doctor."

This isn't the first time I've heard about Granny being able to detect illness. I'd even experienced it myself. Granny predicted my chicken pox two days before I started to show any symptoms. She's also famous for putting her hand on pregnant women's bellies and being able to tell if the baby is a boy or a girl. "It's amazing what Granny can tell just by touching a person," I say.

"It sure is," Daisy says. "And I know some folks'd say your granny's powers come from the devil. But if you ask me, she's an angel straight from heaven."

"Miranda?" I turn around to see Adam standing in the doorway with Dr. So.

"Well, looky there," Daisy says. "It's that sweet little Chinese boy that comes to read me the paper."

I decide to let the "Chinese" thing go. Granny says it's not polite to correct old people, and that probably goes double for sick old people in the hospital. "Adam's a friend of mine from school," I tell Daisy.

"Well, why don't you go play with your little friend while me and Daisy sit a spell?" Granny says. "You can come back and get me in half an hour."

"Okay, Granny," I say.

"Besides," Granny says, "I've got a few things I want to say to Dr. So about Daisy's treatment."

Dr. So looks like a trapped animal as Adam and I leave him.

In Dr. So's office which is full of medical books with disgusting full-color photos we pull up two chairs to the computer. "We need to do a search," Adam says, pulling up a screen. "What words should we search for?"

"How about Charlie Thomas?" I say.

"You've not done many searches, have you?" Adam says. "There are probably ten million people named Charlie Thomas."

"My family doesn't even have a phone. Why would I know anything about internet searches?"

"Hmm..." Adam says. "Let's try 'Charlie Thomas' and 'Wilder' and 'Kentucky.'"

He types the words in, and a list of articles appears on the screen. The first one is titled 'Unsolved Murders.'

When he pulls up the article it says, "Although the Wilder murder case was allegedly 'solved' by the arrest and conviction of Charlie Thomas, many legal experts have suggested that Thomas was probably not the guilty party. Thomas, an African-American youth who may have simply been in the wrong place at the wrong time, could very well have been a victim of the hostile racial climate of the South in the first half of the twentieth century."

"Interesting," Adam says.

"Yeah, interesting, but not helpful. We already know from the writing on the mirror that Charlie T is innocent. This doesn't tell us anything we don't know."

"Well, then..." Adam clicks back to the screen we were on before. "Let's see what else we've got."

A website called 'Shadow World' a Guide to America's Most Haunted Houses' has a short article about the Jameson place: "The so-called Jameson House in Wilder, Kentucky, has sat empty for years because it is supposedly haunted by the ghosts of two sisters who were brutally murdered there by a young man named Charlie Thomas. Some locals claim to have heard ghostly bloodcurdling screams echoing from the abandoned mansion."

"Funny that the real estate agent never mentioned that

when she was showing us the house," Adam says. "Those bloodcurdling ghostly screams would've been a real selling point."

"But you never have heard screams, have you?"

"Nope. A bump in the night once in a while but no screams. The screams must just be a story the people in Wilder made up...like the ones about you being the daughter of Satan."

I laugh. "Shoot, I've not even heard that one."

"No kidding? That's one of the first things I heard about you. That's why you don't have a dad around, you know. He's busy running things down in hell. Some people say your Granny paired off with Satan, too, and that's where your mom came from."

"Really, could people be dumber?" I look at the list of articles, and a name jumps out at me' 'Charlie Thomas, Jr.'

"Hey," I say, "look at this one."

"It's just a website advertising some restaurant," Adam says.

"Look at it," I say. "I've got a feeling about it."

He clicks on it. "Whatever you say, Daughter of Satan."

The screen opens with a cartoon smiling spider that spins a web that spells out the words:

The Café Anansi
African Cuisine and Southern Soul Food
Charlie Thomas, Jr., Proprietor

"I told you," Adam says. "It's just advertising a restaurant."

"But look where the restaurant is," I say. "1616 Rose Street, Lexington, Kentucky. Adam, the man who runs this restaurant is Charlie Thomas's son."

"Like I said, there are probably ten million guys named

Charlie Thomas. How do you know this one is Charlie T's son?"

I can't really explain how I know, except to say that when you have the Sight, sometimes the truth hits you and lights up your brain like fireworks. "Adam, I just know."

He doesn't say anything at first, but when he looks at me I can see he believes me. Then his eyes light up. "Hey," he says. "Dad has a conference in Lexington Saturday after next. Mom and I were going to go with him to do some shopping. Why don't you ask your mom and Granny if you can come with us? The site for this restaurant says it's right next to UK, which is where Dad's conference is. Maybe we could go there and talk to Mr. Thomas."

"Maybe," I say, "but we'll have to be careful. I would think that if your dad was accused of murder, you'd be pretty sensitive about it, and you might be a little freaked out if these kids you didn't know came up to you and wanted to ask you about it."

"You're probably right," Adam says. Then he grins. "That's why I'm going to let you do all the talking."

Chapter Eight

I can't get over how nice the Sos' car is. The back seat, where I'm sitting with Adam, is covered with spotless tan upholstery and is softer than my bed. The stereo system fills the car with classical music. As the violins swell, my stomach flip-flops. I'm excited. I don't get to travel much.

Other than an occasional trip with Mom to Berea to visit some of her old college friends, we don't stray much past Wilder and the nearby, slightly bigger town of Morgan. When I beg Mom to take me to Lexington, she always says, "Hm, I don't trust my old rattletrap of a car enough to drive it that far away from home."

But that's not the real reason. All I had to do was look in Mom's eyes to see into her mind where the truth hid. Lexington was where she lived with my dad, was where they lived when he died, so going there and seeing things like their old apartment building and the pizza place where they used to eat hurts too much. Seeing the big hospital downtown where the doctor said "I'm sorry; it's too late to save him" hurts most of all.

But I want to see where Mom and Dad lived, so I can imagine the times and places they were happy together. I want to make sense of the past.

Lexington probably doesn't look like a big city to people who are used to Louisville or Atlanta, but to me it looks huge. The buildings are way taller than any of the buildings in Wilder or Morgan, and here near the university there are book stores and music stores and restaurants advertising Japanese, Indian and Mexican food. I like it here. When I see a window with a spider design and *The Cafe Anansi* painted on it, I nudge Adam and point it out to him.

Mrs. So drops Dr. So at the building where his meeting is. "We'll come get you at one-thirty," she says. Then she turns to us and asks, "Well, are you ready to shop?"

Mrs. So finds a parking space on the street. "So," she says, once we're out of the car, "where do you kids want to go? I don't care where else I go as long as I get to the Oriental Market."

Adam winces. "Uh-oh. I smell kimchee in our future."

"What's kimchee?" I ask.

"You're lucky not to know," Adam says. "It's this rotted cabbage stuff Koreans like to eat. Mom and Dad can't get enough of it."

Mrs. So gives her son a playful shove. "It's fermented cabbage, not rotted cabbage, and it's very good. And I would rather eat kimchee any day than your American hot dogs. At least I know what's in kimchee." She feeds some coins into the parking meter. "So where do you want to go? I'm sure Adam wants to go to that place that sells used movies."

"Yeah," Adam says. "I thought I might take Miranda there and to a couple of other places. Maybe we could go to a couple of other stores while you shop at the Oriental Market. We could meet you at the car at noon."

Mrs. So purses her lips. "I don't know. Do you think it would be safe?"

"It's broad daylight," Adam says, "and we're not little kids."

"No," Mrs. So sighs, "I guess you're not my little baby anymore." She winks at me. "But he'll always be my little baby, really."

I smile at her, feeling Adam's embarrassment. "Go on," she says after thinking a minute. "But be careful. And have a good time."

The sign on the Cafe Anansi's door says it doesn't open until eleven, so we kill some time at a store next door that sells used paperback books, music, and movies. I buy a couple of books, a mystery for me and one of those stupid teen romances that Abigail likes to read, and Adam gets all excited because he finds a copy of "Daughter of Dracula" on DVD.

When we walk out of the store, the sign on the Cafe, Anansi's door says 'Open.'

It's a small restaurant, shiny clean, with African masks and carvings on the wall. A man in an orange and green loose-fitting shirt who looks like he's around my mom's age is standing behind the cash register. "Can I help you folks?" he says.

"Uh, yes. We'd like two Cokes and," I scan the menu on the wall looking for something that we can both pronounce and afford,"and two pieces of sweet potato pie."

"Coming right up." Moments later, he sets two cans of coke and two paper plates of pie on the counter. "That'll be five dollars even."

As I hand him the money, I say, "Are you Mr. Thomas?"

"Sure am," he says, grinning. "Who wants to know?"

"I'm Miranda Jasper, and this is my friend Adam. We're from Wilder."

"Wilder?" His smile shuts off like somebody flipped a switch.

"Yessir," I say. "Do you know it?"

Mr. Thomas shakes his head. "I reckon you know I know it, or you wouldn't be asking me. What did you do, wake up this morning and decide you wanted to get a look at the son of the man who killed those women back in the day?"

"Your dad wasn't a murderer, Mr. Thomas," I say. "We know that, and we'd like other people to know it, too."

Mr. Thomas wipes a counter that isn't dirty. "Well, young lady, it seems to me you're about seventy years too late to do any good. My daddy served thirty years of hard time for a crime he didn't commit. By the time he got out and got a job and got married, he was older than I am now... too old to be just starting out in life and too scarred to put the pain of the past thirty years behind him. He had had his life taken away from him, and even with a wife and son who loved him, he never got it back. So unless you and your friend can travel back in time, I don't reckon there's much you can do to make a difference."

Half of me wants to turn around and walk out, but the braver half of me says, "What if we proved he was innocent and cleared his name so he wouldn't go down in history as a murderer? Would that make a difference? At least to you?"

Mr. Thomas shrugs. "Maybe to me; I don't know. But it's not like you kids are gonna be able to figure this out. You're what, ten years old?"

"Eleven," Adam says, sounding offended.

"Oh, I beg your pardon, then," Mr. Thomas says, laughing. "That gives you one more full year of investigative experience."

"Mr. Thomas," I say, deciding to take a risk since we've got nothing to lose, "You might think I'm crazy for saying this, but I'm not like other eleven-year-old girls. I...I can see things."

Mr. Thomas raises an eyebrow. "What kind of things?"

"I have the Sight. Well, that's what everybody in my family calls it. But you could also call it being psychic or having ESP. All the women in my family have it. My mom, my granny."

"They live in Wilder too?" Mr Thomas asks.

"Yessir. My granny's name is Irene Chandler, but her maiden name was Stone. Her mother had the Sight, too. She lived out in the woods near Wilder and made potions and tonics for people."

"Huh," Mr. Thomas says. "Your granny's mama, she wasn't the one they called the Witch Woman, was she?"

I grin. "That was her. Of course, they call Granny and Mom both that now."

"My daddy used to tell me a story," Mr. Thomas says, "about his little baby cousin. The baby was real sick, wouldn't eat or move his bowels, and the doctor told the family there wasn't anything he could do; they just had to let nature take its course. Well, the family wasn't gonna give up that easily, so they took the baby to this old lady everybody called the Witch Woman that lived out in the woods. She gave the baby some kind of tonic, and it fixed him right up."

"That would've been my great-grandmother," I say. "So do you think, out of respect to her, you might talk to us a little?"

"Well, I don't know that my talking to you will do much good," Mr. Thomas says, "but I don't guess it'll do any harm either." He glances down at his watch. "Lunch rush won't start for another twenty minutes. Sit on down."

The three of us sit down at a table, and I take a bite of my pie. The crust is buttery and flaky, and the filling is sweet and spicy at the same time. "This pie is great," I say.

Mr. Thomas smiles. "My mama's recipe. All the American food I cook here I learned how to make from my mama. My mother was from Wilder, too. She was one of the folks who got forced onto the trains the night of the murder. She was just a girl, not much older than you. She ended up here in Lexington with her parents. Every week she'd write my dad in jail and tell him she loved him and she'd wait for him. She waited thirty years even though he begged her to find somebody else, he said thirty years was too long to ask somebody to wait. When they finally got married, Mama thought she was too old to have a baby, but well, here I am. A miracle, she always called me. But I'm getting ahead of myself. You wanted to hear about the murder."

"Yessir," I mutter around a mouthful of pie. Adam, I notice, has already polished his off.

"Well," Mr. Thomas says, "Daddy always said he didn't do it, that he didn't have a reason to do it. He said the Jameson sisters were good to him. They gave him little jobs around their house and paid him better than most white folks would. He was delivering the sisters' newspaper when it happened. He said Mildred Jameson had asked him in to move a piece of furniture for her, and a white man was in the living room with Helen. After that, he said, his memory always got foggy.

There was yelling and a struggle and two gunshots. And

then the white man fetched him a blow to the head with a poker that knocked him out cold on the living room floor."

The black hand prints on Adam's living room wall flash into my mind. If Charlie T was knocked in the back of the head, he could have fallen into the wall, bracing his hands against it as he slid to the floor. His hands would have been black with the newsprint from the papers he had been delivering. "I know just where he fell," I say.

"So." Adam finally finds his voice. "If Charlie T saw the man who shot the Jameson sisters and hit him in the head, why didn't he tell the police?"

Mr. Thomas smiles, but it's not a happy smile, exactly. "You kids today can't understand what it was like back then. Nobody would have believed my daddy's word over a white man's. Before the white boy knocked my daddy out, he told him, 'If you say one word about what really happened, you won't live long enough to go to trial, and your mama won't live long enough to cry at your funeral. You say you did it, you'll serve your time and live to be an old man. If you say I did it...well, accidents happen all the time, now don't they? And wouldn't it be a shame if one of them happened to your mama or daddy or sister?'"

My eyes are wet with tears of anger, and when I look at Adam, his are, too. "But he never told you the white boy's name?"

Mr. Thomas shakes his head. "No, he never did, no matter how much I begged him. He said he didn't want me to take it in my head to go and get revenge on that man. He said if I tried to, I'd just wind up in jail myself. Daddy said the best way I could make up for what happened to him was to stay in school and make something out of my life."

I look around the spotless restaurant. "And you did."

Mr. Thomas nods. "Yes, I did. And Daddy got to see

me graduate from college before he died, which he said was the proudest day of his life. He seemed almost happy that day."

"Just almost?" Adam says.

"Almost was as close to happy as he ever got," Mr. Thomas says. "How could he be happy when he had had so much of his life taken away from him? When his good name was ruined forever? It gnawed at him, just like it still gnaws at me. Because of what they did to him, Daddy was never at peace. Even when he died, he wasn't at peace."

"Your dad never dropped any hints about who the killer could have been?" I ask.

"Never did. I remember once, though, Mama let it slip that the boy who did it was the son of some big man on the Wilder City Council at the time the murder happened. No colored person stood a chance in the face of power like that, she said. But Daddy shushed her before she could say anything else."

"Well, that gives us something to go on anyway," I say.

Mr. Thomas smiles and shakes his head. "If you kids want to, you can look up the names of all the government officials in Wilder back then and see which ones of them had sons. Probably most of them did. But you're not gonna get far with this. Everybody involved in the case is probably long dead. And you know what they say, 'Dead men tell no tales.'"

I think of my conversations with Abigail and of the Jameson sisters' messages in Adam's house. "But dead girls do."

Mr. Thomas squints at me. "Has anybody ever told you you're a very strange little white girl?"

I smile. "All the time."

Chapter Nine

"I can't believe how much fun this is." Abigail is sitting cross-legged on top of the dresser in my room playing a game on Adam's Gameboy. "Honestly, Adam, you don't know how lucky you are to have such wonderful things to play with. When I was alive people's idea of a fun toy was a hoop and a stick."

Adam is staring in Abigail's direction, his mouth hanging open. To his eyes, it must look like his Gameboy is floating in a cloud of gray mist, playing itself. "Next time I come I'll bring my laptop. You can play games on it, and it's got a DVD player if you'd like to watch a movie."

Abigail looks up, her eyes wide with excitement. "A movie! Oh, Miranda, I like your friend. It's ever so much more entertaining with him around."

I laugh. "You only like him because he's got better toys than I do."

"Well," Abigail looks up from her game. "He could hardly have worse ones." The Gameboy plays a mournful song, and she looks back down at it. "Oh, no. I died. The story of my life."

I nudge Adam. "You can see why it didn't make any sense to me the first time I heard the expression 'silent as the dead.'"

Abigail loads another cartridge into the Gameboy. "People who think the dead are silent are very poor listeners."

"Hey," Adam says suddenly. "That just made me think of something. Abigail, since you live in the world of the dead, why can't you just find Charlie T and ask him who killed the Jameson sisters?"

"It's not that simple," I mutter, knowing exactly what Abigail is about to say.

"You living," Abigail starts, like I knew she would, " you always think that the world of the dead is about the same size as Wilder...that it's the easiest thing in the world to just look somebody up. But the world of the dead is much, much bigger than the world of the living. Think about all the generations of people who lived out their lives, all the centuries that passed before the current generation of the living was even born. All those people who came before are now in the world of the dead. Our world has a much larger population than yours. Plus, we're all spirits there with no real bodies or addresses. We're very hard to look up."

"There is no Yellow Pages of the dead," I add. "For years I pestered Abigail to find my dad, but she never could. I think our only hope of figuring out who the killer was is to do regular old research. We need to find out who was on the City Council when the murder happened. Then we need to find out which of the city councilmen had sons."

"But what if Mr. Thomas is right?" Adam says. "What if everybody who was involved turns out to be dead?"

"Then," I sigh, "I guess we'll never know, and your house will keep right on being haunted."

Adam's hands flutter in frustration. "But what about that ESP thing you have? Can't you figure out who did it that way?"

"I don't know," I say. "I can look at people and see things about them sometimes, but except for seeing Abigail, I don't have any special powers when it comes to seeing dead people."

"But," Abigail says, setting down the Gameboy suddenly. "If the man who did it is still alive, when you see him, you'll know."

"What will I know?"

"You'll know he is the murderer," Abigail says. "You'll feel it in your blood."

"Abigail," Adam says, "how do you know she'll know?"

"Because I understand the Sight," Abigail says. "When I was alive, I had it, too."

"I don't know why I bother to watch horror movies anymore," Adam says. "I'm living in one."

After Adam begged her and promised to do a lot of chores around the house, Mrs. So agreed to drive us to the public library in Morgan where they keep old copies of area newspapers. I figure if they have issues of *The Wilder Herald* that are old enough, I should be able to find out who was on the City Council the year the Jameson sisters were killed.

"I can't believe this is the main library for the whole county," Adam says as we pull into the parking lot in front of the one-story, shoebox-shaped building.

"It's quite a bit smaller than the library we used to go to in Philadelphia, isn't it, Adam?" Mrs. So laughs.

"But it's still a lot bigger than the library in Wilder," I say.

"I didn't know there was a library in Wilder," Adam says.

"Well, not much of one. It's in the courthouse in a room about the size of your bathroom."

The Morgan County library actually looks pretty big to me, but I'm not sophisticated like the Sos.

Once we're inside, Mrs. So asks, "So where do you want to go 'juvenile fiction?'"

"Actually," Adam says, "we need to look at some old issues of *The Wilder Herald*. It's for a project we're working on."

I notice Adam doesn't say we're working on a school project so, technically, I guess he's not lying.

"Well," Mrs. So says, "then I guess we'd better find a librarian to help us."

"What year of the Herald were you looking for?" a dark-haired man in a black turtleneck at the "help" desk says.

"Nineteen thirty-four," I say.

"Hmm," he frowns. "All the really old issues of the newspapers are on microfilm, but I can find them for you and show you how to use the equipment."

"Oh, I know how," Mrs. So says. "I'm a librarian. Or at least I used to be."

The man behind the desk smiles. "Well, it's always nice to meet a fellow bookworm. I'm Dominick, by the way."

Mrs. So holds out her hand for him to shake. "I'm Pat."

"Well, Pat," Dominick says, "let me scurry off and get the microfilm, and then I'll leave things in your capable hands."

A few minutes later, Mrs. So sits down and loads the microfilm into the projector. Adam and I look over her shoulders. "I didn't know you were a librarian, Mrs. So," I say. She seems more comfortable and relaxed here than I've ever seen her.

"Oh, yes," Mrs. So says. "I worked in the university library the whole time Adam's dad was in medical school.

I'm much better suited for library work than housework, I'm afraid. Staying home all the time is hard for me. "Research like this, though," she says, nodding at the screen, "is fun. So... what are we looking for?"

"The names of all the Wilder City Council members in nineteen thirty-four," I say.

"Okay." Mrs. So scans down the newspaper's pages. "Let's see what we've got."

Finally on page three, we find an article about a City Council meeting. The last two sentences tell us what we need to know: 'City Council members Jack Davis, Smiley Fletcher, Eugene Portwood, Harold Buchanan, Ancil Douglas, and Floyd Silcox were present. City Council member Bill Bradley was absent.'

Yes!" I say, too loud for the library. "Okay, let me copy those names down."

"That was easy," Mrs. So says. "What else do you need to find out for your project?"

"Well..." Adam says, "Is there any way we could look up who on the City Council had children and which ones of them had sons?"

Mrs. So turns around in her chair and looks at Adam. "This strikes me as a very peculiar school project. What exactly is the assignment?"

When I look at Adam's startled face I can see right into his mind. He's thinking, should I come up with a story, or should I tell the truth? He's searching his brain for some kind of convincing story, but he can't find one. Finally, he says, "Well, I never said it was a school project. It's just sort of a project Miranda and I are working on...for fun."

"No offense, my darling son," Mrs. So says. "But I've never known you to go to the library and research something for fun. It's all horror movies and video games with you."

"Well..." Adam shrugs. "Maybe Miranda is a good

influence on me."

"Maybe," Mrs. So says, but she looks suspicious. "So what is this little piece of history you're researching?"

When Adam looks at me, his thoughts say, might as well tell her.

"It's a murder," I say, "a murder that happened in Wilder in nineteen thirty-four."

"In our house," Adam adds.

"In our house?" Mrs. So says, much too loud for inside the library.

In a whisper, I tell Mrs. So everything we know about the murder of the Jameson sisters, ending with, "And we don't think the kid who went to jail for the crime actually did it. We think the killer was the son of one of the City Council members, and we want to prove it."

"Isn't this kind of dangerous taking on a murder investigation?" Mrs. So asks.

"Not when the murder happened seventy years ago," I say. "The guy who did it probably isn't even alive."

"So why bother figuring it out if nobody who was there is even alive?" Mrs. So says.

"Mom." Adam rests his hand on his mother's shoulder. "You'll probably think I'm crazy for saying this, but something isn't right in our house. Miranda and I want to try to fix it."

"Yes," Mrs. So says, covering Adam's hand with her own. "I know what you mean." She doesn't look up but stares down at her and her son's hands. "Sometimes during the day when I'm alone in the house I feel like I'm not really alone, you know? There are sounds sometimes bumping and thumping, nothing you couldn't reason away as the wind or mice in the attic, but still...there's this feeling...an unhappy feeling." She hugs herself like she's cold. "And when I feel it, it makes me unhappy, too." She looks up, right into Adam's eyes. "But Adam, you can never tell your father anything about this, or he'll think we're both crazy."

"I won't tell," Adam says.

"Miranda," says Mrs. So, "you seem to come from a long line of people who are wise about the supernatural. Do you think that if we found out who killed the Jameson sisters, this...presence would leave our house?"

"I think the chances of that are very good," I say.

"Well, then." Mrs. So smiles. "How would you like to have a professional librarian to help you with the rest of your research?"

Chapter Ten

Over the past five days, Mrs. So has proved herself to be a heck of a librarian. When Adam and I sit down at his kitchen table in front of a plate of oatmeal cookies, Mrs. So sits down across from us and pulls out a huge stack of notes. "I went to the courthouse today," she says. "The deeds and records office. I looked up the different City Council members to see who inherited their property when they died. I thought that was the easiest way to figure out who had sons."

Adam grins. "Wow, Mom, that was really smart."

Mrs. So smiles back at him. "I'm good for something besides baking cookies." She flips open a page of notes. "This is what I found, but bear in mind that it's not perfect. If one of these guys had a son who died young or got disinherited, we'd have no way of knowing about it."

I look down at her list:

Wilder City Council Members, 1934

Jack Davis' two daughters, no sons

Eugene Portwood'two sons, Eugene Jr. and Roy, and one daughter

Smiley Fletcher'no children (property left to church)

Harold Buchanan'one son, Harold Jr. and one daughter

Bill Bradley'two sons, William Jr. and Robert, and two daughters

Ancil Douglas' four daughters

Floyd Silcox'one son, Floyd Jr.

"Whoa," Adam says, "so this means our killer could be any one of," he counts the sons' names on the list, "six people."

"Not necessarily," Mrs. So says. "Remember, if the killer was disinherited or died before his father did, I wouldn't have been able to find his name."

"Also..." I stop to think for a second. "I bet some of these councilmen's kids were too young to have committed the crime. Mr. Thomas said his dad described the killer as a young white man, so that would make him a teenager, at least." I look down at my list. "Like, it couldn't be Roy Portwood he's the editor of *The Wilder Herald*, and he's several years younger than Granny. He was just a baby when the murder happened."

"So we can mark him off the list," Adam says, "unless you think a killer baby is a possibility."

"I think we can mark him off," I say, "but we shouldn't mark off his brother Eugene. I don't know anything about him."

"Anybody else on there who's too young?" Adam asks.

"I don't know for sure," I say. "We ought to ask Granny. She probably knows most of these people."

Adam is already up from the table. "Mom, can I go with Miranda to talk to her granny?"

Mrs. So shakes her head, smiling. "Be back by six."

Adam is out the front door with me scrambling behind him.

We find Granny in the kitchen boiling up a nasty mixture of herbs on the stove. "Hidy, younguns," she says. "Stinks to high heaven in here, don't it?"

Adam peers into the pot. "I was just about to say I hope that isn't your dinner on the stove."

"No, just one of my herb teas," Granny says. "You ought to take you a jar home and let your daddy try it. He might want to use it on some of his patients. It smells rotten, but it's the best thing in the world to keep you regular."

I shoot Adam a look that means *don't go there*. "Granny," I say, "do you remember me asking you about the Jameson murders?"

"Of course I remember. I ain't that far gone yet."

"Well, we've got a list of possible suspects we want you to take a look at."

Granny cackles. "Listen at you! A list of possible suspects! You read too many of them mystery stories." She turns off the stove and sits down at the kitchen table. "Well, set down and show it to me." She puts her reading glasses on her pointy nose.

"What we need to know," Adam says, "is which of these city councilmen's kids would have been teenagers or older in nineteen thirty-four."

"Well, now, let me see..." Granny looks down her nose through her glasses. "Eugene Portwood would've been seventeen or eighteen back in thirty-four. He died a few years back. His brother run a big story about him in the paper."

"What was he like?" I ask.

"I didn't know much but his name, he was so much older than me," Granny says. "But everybody always said the Portwoods was good folks." She looks back down at the list. "Now Harold Buchanan Jr., he's about the same age as Eugene Jr., but he's still alive. You'd probably know him if you was to see him, Miranda. He was on the City Council for years himself, and his boy, Harold III, is a state senator now."

"What's he like?" I ask.

"I couldn't tell you," Granny says. "Like most folks in this town, he always took off running the other way when he saw me coming." She traces a line down the list with her gnarled index finger. "Now Bobby Bradley is a year or two younger than me, so he was pretty little when it happened. His brother, Bill Jr., would've been fifteen or sixteen. And Bill Jr. was a mess, let me tell you. Always getting in trouble for things like painting dirty words on the walls in the high school or tying tin cans to some old dog's tail. I can't say I ever cared much for Bill. Of course, there's a big line between pranks such as his and murder."

"Is he still alive?" Adam asks.

"He is," Granny says. "He retired from the hardware store over in Morgan a few years back.

He's a crotchety an old coot as you're ever likely to meet." She looks back down the list. "Now Floyd Silcox Jr. moved off years ago, and I never heard what happened to him. I'd be surprised if he was still alive, though. He was always a sickly type, even as a youngun. His ma used to come to my ma to get remedies for his breathing troubles."

"How old would he have been in nineteen thirty-four?" I ask.

"Fifteen or sixteen," Granny says, "but weak as the little feller always was, I doubt he would've had the strength to pull the trigger."

"So," I say, "I guess our main suspects are Eugene Portwood, Harold Buchanan, Bill Bradley, and maybe Floyd Silcox if his health got better."

"Hm," Adam says, "I wonder if Bill Bradley and Harold Buchanan are listed in the phone book."

"Why?" Granny says. "So you can call them up and ask them if they killed a couple of ladies in nineteen and thirty-four?" She reaches out and grabs my hand, then Adam's and holds them. "Listen, younguns, I think this has gone far enough. There's somebody out there who don't like you digging all this dirt back up I don't know who it is, but I know he don't like it. And I know he ain't somebody you'd want to cross. I know finding out all this stuff has been exciting, and I know you feel like figuring it out is gonna right a wrong that was done seventy years ago. But maybe it's too late to right that wrong."

"But maybe it's not," I say. "What about clearing Charlie T's name? That would mean a lot to his family. And what about the spirits of the Jameson sisters? Maybe once Charlie T is cleared, they can be at peace."

"That's another thing that worries me," Granny says. "The spirits of the Jameson sisters. Have you ever stopped to think that they might not be good spirits? Maybe getting murdered turned them all bitter and mean...old Mildred was pretty bitter and mean to start with. Maybe they're just pretending to need your help so they can lead you to danger."

"Man," Adam says, "that's sure gonna make me feel safe in my bed tonight."

"Well, if safe is how you want to feel," Granny says, "then you ought to give up this whole business." She looks hard at Adam and me with her dark, sharp eyes that always remind me of a crow's.

"Now I want you'uns to promise you'll think about what I

said."

"I promise," I say.

"I promise," Adam says, too.

But as soon as we've excused ourselves and gone outside, Adam whispers, "I'll check to see if any of those guys are in the phone book."

"Okay," I say, "but don't call anybody without me."

I know that if Granny says we're in danger, then we're in danger. But I also know that I can't stop now. Giving up now would be like getting woken up from a really exciting dream by the buzz of the alarm clock, when you know it's going to drive you crazy because you'll never know how the story ended.

Right before the bell is about to ring, I run up to Adam at his locker. His hair is sticking up funny, and his eyes look puffy, but that's not unusual for him in the morning. "Hey," I say, "did you find anybody's name in the phone book?"

"Yeah," he says, but he doesn't sound excited like I thought he would. "Bill Bradley and Harold Buchanan are both in the phone book. But that's not the main thing on my mind right now."

"Well, then, what is?"

Adam opens his locker, takes out an envelope, and hands it to me. "This is."

The envelope is addressed to Mrs. Pat So. Mrs. So's name and address have been typed, and there is no return address. I take the paper out of the envelope. The letter is just one typed sentence: *Mind your own business.*

Chapter Eleven

I don't even bother unwrapping my sandwich at lunch. I'm too upset to eat.

"Mom won't help us anymore," Adam says. "She says she has to think of Dad and his job and our family that we have to find a way of fitting into this community. She says she can't afford to do anything that might make the people in Wilder turn against us. I told her that in that case, we'd better figure out some way to stop being Asian, but she didn't think that was funny." He looks down at his tray. He hasn't touched his lunch either.

"I understand what she means, I guess. If she makes enemies here, nobody will want your dad to be their doctor."

"Yeah," Adam says. "And she doesn't want me making enemies either. She told me to forget about the Jameson murder, that I ought to be spending more time on my schoolwork and less time trying to change something that it's too late to change."

"But what about the spirits in your house, the weird noises and the hand prints? Doesn't she at least want to fix that?"

Adam rolls his eyes. "Mom has convinced herself or maybe she let Dad convince her that there aren't really any spirits. She says the sounds were probably just the mice in the attic, and the weird feelings she had were just because she hasn't adjusted to the move yet. And the handprints... well, maybe she just hasn't found the right kind of cleaner to remove that stain."

I put my uneaten sandwich back into my lunch bag. I'd offer it to one of the poor kids, but nobody will take food from the witch girl. "Do you think she really believes all that?"

Adam is quiet for a few seconds. "I think she really wants to believe it because the only other choice is to be afraid."

A terrible thought pops into my head, so terrible I almost can't make myself say it. "Adam, does your mom want you to...stop being friends with me?"

"Oh, no," Adam says. "Mom likes you. She thinks you've gotten a little too caught up in the whole Nancy Drew thing, but she still thinks you're a nice kid. She says you're welcome to come over any time to play games or watch movies. She just wants us to give up this...obsession, she calls it."

I look into Adam's eyes and then into his mind and see that it's just as full of questions and ideas about the Jamesons as mine is. "You don't want to give up, do you?" I say.

"No," Adam says. "Not when we're so close to an answer. But I also don't want to get in trouble."

"Well," I say, "we'll just have to be extra careful then."

This afternoon we're pretty well covered because I told Mom I might be going over to Adam's house after school, and he told his mom he might be coming to my house. For once, I'm grateful that my family doesn't have a phone.

"So," Adam says, as we walk toward downtown, "what's the plan?"

"I thought we might go by the Wilder Herald office and see Roy Silcox," I say. "Maybe ask him a few questions about his brother."

"What, like did your older brother ever strike you as the cold-blooded murderer type?"

"Oh, I think we can be a little smoother than that."

The lady at the front desk at the Herald office looks up at us through cat's eye glasses that were in style back when my mom was a little girl (I know this because there's a picture of Mom when she was younger than me wearing glasses just like this lady's). "Are you kids selling something for school?" she asks.

"No, ma'am," I say. "We'd like to talk to Mr. Silcox."

"Well, Mr. Silcox is a busy man." The lady's hair looks like a hard gray helmet. A pencil sticks out of it like an antenna. All of a sudden she yells back to the office, "Roy! There's some kids here to see you! You want to talk to them?"

"Send 'em on back," a man's voice calls.

"Third door on your left," she says.

Mr. Silcox's office is small and cluttered with papers, half-empty coffee cups, and overflowing ashtrays. Mr. Silcox is leaning back in the chair at his desk, his glasses pushed up to rest on top of his bald head. His eyes look droopy, like he's just been woken up from a nap, which, I think, is what we've just done.

"Hello, young folks, come on in and sit down," he says.

"You'll have to excuse the mess. My wife comes in here with a bulldozer once a month and cleans this place up, but that time of month hasn't rolled around yet."

We sit down in the chairs across from his desk. His tie, I notice, is untied and stained, and I can see patches of his round white belly peeking between the buttons of his dingy shirt.

"So," he says, "what can I do for you young people?"

I look at Adam, whose lips are clamped shut. Clearly, I'm going to have to do all the talking. "Well, sir," I say, "we're working on a project about the history of Wilder. And we were wondering if we could maybe interview you."

Roy Silcox chuckles. "Figured an old coot like me might be able to tell you what you want to know, huh? Well, I'm always happy to help out young reporters such as yourselves. Go ahead fire away."

"Okay," I say, not sure what to say next because I didn't really plan out any questions. "What was it like living in Wilder when you were a kid?"

"Well," he says, chewing on his cigar, "you kids would probably think it was right boring because you've got all your ready-made entertainment now, TV and computer games and what have you. But we didn't have any of that, so we had to make our own fun playing ball, fishing, riding our bikes all over town. And I'll tell you what: we were never bored. Me, my brother Eugene, the boys we ran around with'we always had something going on."

He looks over our shoulders for a minute, as though he's looking into his own past. "Of course," he says, "back then it was different. The world wasn't as dangerous as it is now, and a little bitty town like Wilder wasn't dangerous at all. Now parents feel like they've got to keep their kids home where they can keep an eye on 'em. But back then shoot, in the summertime, we'd get on our bikes after breakfast, take off somewhere, and not come back till suppertime."

"And your mom didn't worry?" I ask.

"No," Mr. Silcox laughs. "Course, she probably should have, given some of the stuff we were getting into, but it was all innocent fun, really. And Ma knew that Wilder was a safe place to run around in, that nobody would bother us."

"So," Adam says, finally deciding to help me out, "there wasn't any crime in Wilder back then?"

"No big crimes," Mr. Silcox says. "Maybe some old boy might get picked up for being drunk and disorderly, or maybe some kids might get in trouble for vandalizing school property, but that was about it."

I figure now is as good a time as any, so I say, "But wasn't there a murder here back in the thirties?"

"Oh," Mr. Silcox says. For a moment, his mouth is clamped shut in a straight line, and I'm afraid he's going to tell us to get out of his office. But then he takes a deep breath and says, "You want to know about the Jameson murder. Now that was a strange thing. People couldn't hardly believe such a thing could happen in Wilder. And to two maiden ladies who wouldn't hurt a fly! Why, Helen Jameson had taught me and Eugene both in grade school, and she was such a sweet little thing. Her sister Mildred was a little crotchety, but she was basically a good woman. Nobody could figure out why somebody would want them dead. When it happened, Eugene had already left home he'd quit school and joined the army. He was over at Fort Campbell doing basic training. Ma sent him a newspaper clipping about the Jamesons, and he wrote back saying he couldn't believe such a thing had happened in the quiet town he had grown up in. He said he didn't know what the world was coming to."

As Mr. Silcox gazes at some faraway moment from the

past, Adam and I catch each other's eye: time to cross Eugene Silcox off our list. "Mr. Silcox,"I say, "did you know the boy who got arrested for the murder?"

"I knew who he was, but of course I wasn't hardly out of diapers when it happened. I knew Charlie T delivered papers and did odd jobs for folks. He seemed like a nice, quiet boy. He never seemed like the type to kill somebody, let alone two white ladies back when black folks were getting such a raw deal. The story went that he was mad at the Jameson sisters because they'd hired some other boy to do their yard work. But it seems like you'd have to have an awfully bad temper to kill somebody over that."

"So you don't think he did it?" I say.

"Most of what I know about the case I learned years after it happened. But no, I don't think the case against him was that strong." He looks at Adam, then at me. "Say...you two are trying to find out all you can about this murder, aren't you? You're trying to figure out who really did it."

I look down, embarrassed for some reason. "Yes, sir. But we'd appreciate it if you didn't tell anybody."

"My lips are sealed," he says, chuckling. "I tell you what. I don't think you kids are gonna get anywhere with this, but I'll make you a deal here and now. If you do find out something big, come and tell me, and I promise you a front-page story in *The Wilder Herald*."

"Thank you, sir." A front-page newspaper story clearing Charlie T would probably be enough to satisfy the Jameson sisters and to give Charlie Thomas, Jr. some satisfaction, too. But we haven't proved a thing yet, and from the sound of his chuckling, Roy Silcox doesn't think we ever will.

As soon as we're out of the office, Adam says, "So unless Mr. Silcox is lying, his brother can't be the killer."

"And I don't think Mr. Silcox is lying," I say. "Having the

Sight makes you pretty good at telling whether somebody's lying or not. That's why I always tell the truth to Mom and Granny. There's no point in lying to somebody who can look right inside your head."

Walking back toward town, Adam pauses in front of the Kwik-E Mart. "Hey," he says, "there's a pay phone here. Why don't we call the other guys who were listed in the phone book?"

I reach inside my skirt pocket. Empty, as usual. "You got any change?"

"Sure," he grins, "I'm a doctor's kid. I'm rich."

The phone book which is attached to the pay phone has been rained on so often it's swollen and its pages are stuck together. Luckily, Wilder is so small that the listings for Bradley and Buchanan are on the same page, which is smeary but still readable. Remembering that Granny described Bill Bradley as a cranky old codger, I decide to dial Harold Buchanan first. Maybe talking to him will be easier.

I feed the money into the phone and punch the numbers, getting ready to make my little speech about how my friend and I are working on a project on the history of Wilder. But when the dial tone stops, what I hear is a robotic-sounding recording that says, "I'm sorry. You have reached a number that has been disconnected or is no longer in use."

"Huh," I say, hanging up. "His number's been disconnected."

"Maybe he didn't pay his phone bill," Adam says.

"Maybe, but from what Granny said he sounds like the bill-paying type. Maybe he moved."

"Could be," Adam says. "Why don't you try Bill Bradley?"

I sigh. "You sure you don't want to try him?"

"Hey, I provide the quarters. You make the phone calls."

"All right."

After three rings a gruff voice says, "Yeah?"

"Um...hello. May I speak to Bill Bradley, please?"

"This is Bill Bradley. Who are you?"

Granny wasn't kidding about him being crotchety. "My name is Miranda Jasper. I'm in sixth grade at Wilder School. My friend Adam and I are working on a project about the history of Wilder, and we thought that since you've lived here all your life, you might be a good person to interview."

"You're the witch woman's granddaughter, ain't you?"

I swallow hard to fight the temptation to hang up on him. "My grandmother is Irene Chandler, if that's who you mean."

"Yeah, that's her. Well, I ain't skeered of her nor you neither."

"And you shouldn't be scared of us, sir. We're nice people."

"Hmf." He's so quiet for a minute I wonder if he's still there, then he says, "So if I was to tell you what I think about Wilder, you'd write it down and use it in your school project?"

"Yes, sir. That's right."

"You know where I live at?"

"Across the street from the Piggly Wiggly, right?"

"That's right. Well, you and your little friend come on over here after you get out of school tomorrow, and I'll tell you what I think of Wilder."

"Thank you, Mr. Bradley. We'll see you then."

"Well," I say, hanging up the phone. "It looks like you're going to have to tell your mom you're coming over to my house tomorrow afternoon."

"Why's that?"

"Because we're going to be paying a visit to Bill Bradley."

Chapter Twelve

Most people in town call the Piggly Wiggly grocery store the Pig. This means it's not weird to hear adults say things like, "We're about out of milk, so I reckon I'd better go to the Pig." The first time Granny heard somebody saying that, she said, "But pig's milk ain't fit to drink. Why don't you let me sell you some goat's milk?"

Right now we're standing in the Pig's parking lot, looking across the street at Bill Bradley's place. It's a small, white, aluminum-sided house with lots of tacky lawn ornaments in its postage-stamp-sized front yard. Green painted concrete frogs sit on a white concrete bench. A little Dutch boy and girl, also concrete, are frozen in a kiss, and a concrete lawn jockey with a black-painted face stands by the front porch holding a lantern.

"If that lawn jockey's any sign," Adam says, "my guess is that Bill Bradley wasn't that broken up about what happened to Charlie T."

"That'd be my guess, too," I say. "So do you have your nerve up to actually go talk to this guy?"

"Sure," Adam says, "as long as you're the one who really does the talking."

We cross the street and walk past all the concrete characters to get to Bill Bradley's front door. When I knock, a deep voice growls, "Who is it?"

"Miranda Jasper," I yell through the door. "We talked on the phone yesterday."

"Come in," the voice yells back.

In the living room, Bill Bradley is sitting in a green recliner. What little gray hair he has is uncombed, and his belly strains against a tight, dingy undershirt which gaps over his faded pajama bottoms. A game show is on the TV, which is turned up so loud I'm surprised he could hear us knocking.

"Sit down," he says, not looking away from the screen. We take a seat on an ugly brown couch which has a picture of a blond-haired Jesus hanging over it. Mr. Bradley picks up the remote control and turns the TV down but not off. "So," he says, "what was it you'uns was wanting me to tell you about Wilder?"

"Well..." I start, "I guess we'd like to hear what it was like living in Wilder when you were a kid...and a teenager."

"Back then," Mr. Bradley says, scratching his belly underneath his shirt, "Wilder was a right nice place to live. Of course, the Depression was on, so people didn't have no money, but times was still better than now 'cause people knew how to act."

"How to act?" I say.

"That's right. Young folks minded their parents. There wasn't no rap music or dope or people getting above themselves. People knew what their place was, and they stayed in it."

I glance at Adam, who looks like he's going to make a run for it. "So," I say to Mr. Bradley, "would you say that Wilder was safer back then?"

"Sure it was safer," Mr. Bradley says. "You could leave your front door open back then."

"But what about that murder?" Adam says. "Those two ladies that got killed in nineteen thirty-four?" I notice that Adam is developing a pattern during our interviews. He sits with his mouth shut while I get the person talking, then finds his voice when he gets impatient to talk about the murder.

"Oh, you wanna hear about that, do you?" Mr. Bradley flips off the tv and for the first time since we've been there, really looks at us. "Now that was one time when somebody did forget what his place was," he says. "But he learned it again real quick."

"Do you mean Charlie Thomas?" I ask.

"If that was the name of the boy that killed the Jameson sisters, then that's who I mean. I don't recollect his name myself."

Hate bubbles and steams from Mr. Bradley like some evil potion boiling in a cauldron. As I look in his head I see a whole catalog of the people he hates: black people, Hispanics, Catholics, Democrats, and a anybody else who's not just like him. His mind is not a fun place to be, and I get out of there as fast as I can. "So," I say, "you think Charlie T did it."

"Of course he did it!" Bill Bradley yells. "He shot them two ladies like they wasn't better than a couple of squirrels. And how come? Because he thought he was entitled to a handout from them that he wasn't getting."

"Where were you when the murder happened?" Adam

asks. His voice is shaking, and his hands are balled into fists.

"Me?" To my surprise, Mr. Bradley smiles. "I was sittin on the porch swing of the old homeplace, with my arm around the girl who was gonna be my wife. That's her picture setting there on top of the TV. She died ten years ago this April."

I look at the picture of the smiling, grandmotherly woman and try to figure out how a man like Bill Bradley can be so full of hate and still have room for love. "She was pretty," I say.

"Prettiest girl I ever seen," Mr. Bradley says. "Anyhow, I was sitting on the porch swing with Betty when one of Daddy's friends came driving up in his car. He hollered for Daddy, and when Daddy come out the feller told him that the colored boy who delivered the paper had just killed both of the Jameson sisters. Well, Daddy was mad enough to spit nails. He was yelling about how no respectable white woman was safe in her own house these days. And that evening Daddy got his gun and said that him and some of the boys was going to the other side of town to teach them a lesson. I begged to go, too, but Daddy said I had to stay home to protect my mama and my sister. I sure was sorry to miss all that excitement, though."

In my mind I see what Mr. Bradley thinks of as excitement: the Klan, which Mr. Bradley's father the city councilman was a member of, burning crosses, firing shots, marching men and women and children onto freight cars and out of town. And all that time, young Bill Bradley sitting on the porch, just like he had been when the Jameson sisters were killed. I can see him there on the porch swing with his brown-haired girlfriend, and I know that no matter how terrible a person he is, he isn't the killer.

"Of course, I don't want you to think I'm prejudiced," Mr. Bradley is saying when I come back to the here and now. Mr. Bradley nods toward Adam. "Like I couldn't help but notice that you're a person of the Oriental persuasion. And I don't have no problem with you people. Now, sure, I killed a few of your kind in the war, but that was different; they wasn't Americans. When you people come over here and decide to be Americans, though, there ain't nobody that works harder than you do. They's a lot of real Americans that could learn a thing or two from your people."

Adam's mouth wouldn't be hanging open any wider if an elephant had just walked into the room. Because I'm not sure if he should say whatever's going to come out of his mouth when he can talk again, I say, "Well, Mr. Bradley, thank you for your time. We'd better be getting home now."

I grab Adam's arm and pull him toward the door.

"Come back any time you want to, young'uns," Mr. Bradley says. "This world'd be a better place if more people your age would take the time to listen to old people."

"Not to old people like him!" Adam spits as soon as we're out the door. "I think he is the very worst person I've ever met in my life."

"Hey, now," I say, nudging Adam. "He doesn't have nothin' against you people."

Adam doesn't even crack a smile.

"I know...he is pretty terrible," I say as we cross the street to the Pig.

"So," Adam says, "should we go ahead and talk to the police, do you think?"

"Why would we do that?"

Adam looks at me like I'm the dumbest person on earth. "To tell them that Bill Bradley killed the Jameson sisters and blamed it on Charlie T."

I stop walking and turn to face him. "But he didn't do it."

"What do you mean he didn't do it?" Adam is yelling. This is the first time he's ever acted mad at me. "You heard him. You heard the way he talked about black people. Do you think he wouldn't have hated Charlie T enough to frame him for the murder?"

"Sure, I think he would've hated Charlie T enough." I'm speaking softly, trying to calm Adam down. "But what reason would he have had for killing a couple of 'respectable white ladies' like Helen and Mildred Jameson? It doesn't make any sense."

"Well," Adam says, like he's stalling for time. "He probably had his reasons. We just need to find out what those reasons were."

Adam starts walking again, but I grab his arm and make him look at me. "Listen," I say. "Bill Bradley is probably pretty high on the list of biggest jerks of all time, but just because he's a jerk, that doesn't make him a murderer. I have the Sight, Adam. I can tell when people are lying, and when Mr. Bradley said he was on the porch swing when the murders happened, he was telling the truth."

"But you said your sight wasn't as strong as your mom's and granny's. Maybe it's not strong enough for you to see that Bill Bradley is lying."

"You could be right," I say, even though I'm sure Mr. Bradley is telling the truth. "But don't you remember what Abigail said? She said when I met the killer I would know... I would feel it.

When I met Bill Bradley I didn't feel anything...except for the feeling that I didn't like him much."

We're walking again, toward downtown. When we pass

the dollar store, Adam says, "So if it's not Bill Bradley and it's not Eugene Silcox, that just leaves us with two guys we don't know anything about, that Floyd guy, who could be anywhere if he's even still alive, and Harold Buchanan, whose phone has been disconnected."

"Maybe we should try to find Harold Buchanan's house and see if it looks like anybody's living there."

"Yeah," Adam says, "but not today. Mom'll get suspicious if I'm home too late."

"Tomorrow, then," I say. We're almost to Adam's house. "You know, it's funny. The name Harold Buchanan sounds really familiar to me...like it's a name I knew before we started looking up all this stuff."

"It's probably not that weird that you've heard of him," Adam says. "Your granny said he used to be a big name in Wilder, and you've lived here all your life."

"That's true." We're standing in front of Adam's big pink house, and I wonder if the ghosts of the Jameson sisters are in there somewhere talking about how they wish the message they'd left on the bathroom mirror could've been read by some people with brains, unlike Adam and me.

"What is weird, though," Adam says, "is that Harold Buchanan's name sounds familiar to me, too, and I hardly know anybody in this town. Maybe it just sounds familiar because it reminds me of James Buchanan, the president I always forget when I try to name all the presidents."

"Could be," I say. "I'm beginning to see why all these grownups have laughed at us for trying to figure this thing out."

Adam shakes his head. "Maybe Mom's right. Maybe you and I need to find another hobby."

The clock says midnight. I've been in bed for two

hours, but I can't get to sleep. My mind keeps trying to put together the jigsaw puzzle of the Jameson murder, but there are too many pieces missing.

When the closet door opens, I'm glad. If I have to be awake, at least I won't be awake alone.

"Oh, for heaven's sake, look at you. You're as wide awake as I am." Abigail jumps onto my bed and sits with her knees hugged to her chest. "I've never been able to figure out why the living use that expression 'sleep like the dead.' We never sleep."

"I guess it's because dead people look like they're asleep," I say.

"Do I look asleep to you?" Abigail says. "You mean dead bodies look asleep, not dead people. The body isn't the person. It's just the container that holds the person until it wears out."

"I guess so," I say.

"You're unhappy. I can tell," Abigail says. She pulls down the covers and crawls into the bed beside me. "Scoot over, will you." She strokes my hair with her fingers, which make it feel like a cool breeze is blowing through my hair. "There's no need to make yourself miserable over something that happened seventy years ago," she says.

"But it's driving me crazy. There's so much we don't know."

"Perhaps people would be better off if they admitted that there's a great deal that they don't know and will never know. You're lucky, though, Miranda. You have the Sight. You get to know more than most people."

"I get to know more than I want to know most of the time," I say. "Maybe that's why I'm so frustrated right now. I'm not used to knowing less than I want to know."

"Well, right now you're probably feeling like most people

feel. Not so wonderful, is it?

Feeling normal?"

"I can't feel that normal. I'm having a slumber party with a ghost." Then, because I can't get his name out of my head, I say, under my breath, "Harold Buchanan."

"What was that?" Abigail says.

"Harold Buchanan he's one of the guys who could have committed the murder. We can't find him, but the thing that's driving me nuts is that his name sounds so familiar to me, and I can't figure out why."

"Hmm." Abigail props up on her elbow. "Maybe he's a friend of your granny's."

"No, Granny doesn't have any men friends. Not that she has many women friends either.

About the only friend she's close to is Daisy'oh!" A picture as clear as a photograph pops into my head.

"What?" Abigail asks.

"I can't believe I didn't think of it til now. That day when I went with Granny to visit Daisy in the hospital...Granny was making me read all the names of the patients on the hall. Harold Buchanan'that was one of the names!" That's where I had heard it before, and that's where Adam knew it from, too. Harold Buchanan was probably one of Adam's father's patients!

Chapter Thirteen

It's ten minutes before school starts, and I'm waiting on the sidewalk outside Adam's house. I've been up for hours, itching to tell him about Harold Buchanan.

Finally Adam stumbles out of the front door, his eyes still sleepy, his hair sticking up from the crown. His backpack is flung over his shoulder, and he has a comb in one hand and a Pop-Tart in the other. I watch him sleepily try to comb his hair with a Pop-Tart before he realizes he's using the wrong hand. "Hello, Mr. Morning Person," I say.

"Miranda!" He stuffs the comb in his pocket and rubs his eyes. "What's up?"

"I figured out where we know the name Harold Buchanan from," I say. "He's a patient at the hospital. He's on the same hall where I ran into you that day I was visiting with Granny."

Adam wags his Pop-Tart in excitement. "Buchanan! Yeah, that's right! That's the name of that old guy who's been in the hospital for months. When I help out Dad he always says not to bother going into his room that the old man's really sick and just needs to rest quietly because he's probably not going to make it too much longer."

"Which is probably why his phone's disconnected," I say. "He knows he's not going home."

"Sad," Adam says, and we walk in silence for a while.

"Yeah. So...do you think it would be really bad if we tried to talk to him?"

"Not necessarily." Adam swings the school door open. "If we caught him sometime when he was awake, he might not mind talking to us. He might even be glad for the company."

"Yeah, but if we go there and he seems too weak to talk, then we should just leave him alone and try to forget about this whole thing. Don't you think?"

"Yeah, we can try to forget it."

We stop at our lockers to get our books. When I open my locker and see what's inside, I choke back a scream.

A black stuffed toy cat is dangling inside my locker with a noose around its neck. Pinned to its chest is a note in bloody red magic marker: CURIOSITY KILLED THE CAT.

"Okay," Adam says, his voice shaky, "that's freaky. I think you'd better tell the principal or the police or somebody."

I take down the cat, throw it in the trash can, and cover it up with papers. "I'm not going to tell the principal or anybody else. Somebody's just trying to scare us, that's all. And I refuse to be scared." But my hands are shaking.

At lunch Adam says, "Look, I've been thinking. Maybe we should just chill out a little while."

"What do you mean, chill out?"

"You know, stop asking questions, stop trying to figure things out. These notes, the one that came to my house, the one just now they're threats, Miranda. And I'm not anywhere near as scared of the ghosts in my house as I am of the person who's sending these notes."

I lean over the table and look right at him. "Don't you see what these notes mean? They mean we're close to the truth, so close that whoever did it is getting scared. Listen, Adam, if you're afraid, if you want to quit, that's fine. I don't blame you, and I won't hold it against you." I lean back in my seat. "And if I have to, I'll go on and figure out this thing without you."

"No!" Adam says, so loud that a few people turn their heads to look at our table. They probably think I'm putting a curse on Adam or something. "If you're not quitting, I'm not either."

"Listen, I was just going to go over to the hospital to see Dad after school today. You wanna come, too? Maybe we can talk to Mr. Buchanan."

I grin. "I'm there."

When we peek into Mr. Buchanan's room, we can tell he's really sick. He is drawn and thin and his skin looks like crumpled up white tissue paper stretched over skull and skeleton. He is connected to tubes and machines that pump him full of medicine and keep track of his heart and breathing. He looks small and alone. Only the flowers and cards on his dresser and bedside table show that there are people who care about him.

I'm surprised when his eyes open. "Young people," he says. His voice is thin and shaky. As soon as his eyes meet mine, I feel like someone hit me, hard, in the back of the head. The pain is so intense I'm afraid I'm going to pass out, but around the pain, I can feel my Sight trying to connect with Mr. Buchanan, trying to get inside his thoughts. But I can't see because I'm blinded by pain and fear.

I don't know how long I've been standing there, hurting and shaking, but once I can focus on something oustside of myself, I hear Adam saying, "I'm Dr. So's son. My friend and I wondered if we could bring you anything to make you more comfortable. Would you like an extra blanket or maybe a drink from the Coke machine?"

"Well..." He glances over at the dresser, "there is a Hershey bar on the dresser, if one of you would bring it to me."

"Well," Adam says, "We'd better move your bed up if you're going to eat something." While Adam fixes the bed, I go get the candy bar off the dresser, but my knees are so weak I can barely walk. I manage to make it over to Mr. Buchanan's bed. When I hold out the candy bar to him in my shaking hand, he says, "No, honey, I'm too weak. You'll have to feed it to me."

My shaky hands make it almost impossible to open the wrapper. "Don't be nervous," Mr. Buchanan says. "I know I don't look too pretty, but I'm perfectly harmless."

Tell that to the Jameson sisters, I think. "I...I just have unsteady hands," I say. "It runs in my family."

Adam gives me a weird look, but I ignore it. "Just break off small pieces for me," Mr. Buchanan says. "I won't be able to eat much."

I break off a tiny piece of chocolate for Mr. Buchanan. He opens his mouth like a baby bird, and I put the candy on his tongue. I want to scream, to cry, to run away, but instead I break off another piece of chocolate.

"Ah," Mr. Buchanan sighs. "Chocolate is still good, even

when you're dying." He lets another piece melt on his tongue. "Pancreatic cancer," he says, looking over at Adam. "Your daddy says I've got maybe three weeks left."

"I'm sorry, sir," Adam says.

"Me, too," Mr. Buchanan says. "I've had a good long run of it, though."

"Yessir," I say, feeding him another bit of chocolate.

"It's strange being so weak," he says. "I was never a weak man. I used to be a powerful man in this town, just like my daddy before me. And my son well, he's a powerful man, period. A state senator. He came down to see me this weekend." He opens his mouth for more chocolate. "Mm," he says. "You know, scientists say the reason people like chocolate is because it makes them feel like they're in love. And love...well, love is even better than power. I know that now."

"Is...is Mrs. Buchanan alive?" I ask.

"No, she's not," he says. "But I wasn't thinking about Mrs. Buchanan just then." He smiles a little. "I shouldn't be saying things like that to you children. You're too young. You'll have to forgive me. My illness makes my mind duller than it used to be. Did you ever tell me your names?"

"Miranda and Adam," I say. I'm less woozy than I was a few minutes ago, but there's a big knot of fear in my stomach.

"Miranda and Adam, Miranda and Adam," Mr. Buchanan says, almost singing. "Wait...Bill Bradley came to see me this morning and told me a girl and a boy came by his house yesterday asking all kinds of questions. A red-haired girl and an Oriental boy...named Miranda and Adam."

Even though I know that lying there in his sickbed, Mr. Buchanan can't do anything to harm us, I feel more afraid than I can ever remember feeling. "Yessir," I manage to choke out, "we're working on a project...for school."

"Well, I would advise you to find another topic for your project," Mr. Buchanan says. "There are certain people in this town who want to make sure that things in the past stay in the past. And I would hate for you children to get into any danger." He looks at Adam, then at me. "Well," he says, "I think I've had enough chocolate. And I'm sure you children will understand if I run you off without answering any of the questions you no doubt wanted to ask me. My future is short, and my past is my business."

"Whoa," Adam says, once we're out in the hall. "I think we made him mad. I feel bad for upsetting him, as sick as he is."

"Adam, it's him."

He looks at me like I'm speaking Russian or something. "What do you mean, it's him?"

"I mean'" I stop for a second, realizing that it might not be a good idea to say what I'm going to say out loud in the middle of the hospital's crowded lobby. I pull Adam out the front door, then whisper, "I mean he's the murderer."

"How do you know?" Adam doesn't sound like he believes me.

"I know because I felt it as soon as he looked at me. That's why I didn't talk at first. I was in too much pain."

"Whoa. You are kind of a spooky girl, aren't you?"

I decide to ignore this comment. "It's just like Abigail said. She said when you meet the murderer, you'll know."

Adam shoves his hands in the pockets of his baggy pants as he walks. "Look, it's great that you know and everything. But it still doesn't do us much good. I mean, are we supposed to convince the police that this sick, old man who used to be one of the people who ran this town is a murderer because of the way he made you feel? We're going to have to get some proof."

"I know," I say, "and that's what worries me. Because I have no idea how we're going to get it."

Chapter Fourteen

Adam's parents said it would be okay for Adam to come over tonight to eat supper and study with me for our history test. We did eat supper, but we're not making great progress studying for our history test, what with questions about Wilder's history weighing on our minds.

The real reason I asked Adam over was in hopes that we could figure out some way to prove Harold Buchanan's guilt. And if Abigail showed up to talk with us, that would be even better. Three heads are better than two, even when one head does belong to a ghost.

"It's just like the Kennedy assassination," Adam is saying, pointing to a page in the history book. "The guy who everybody said was the murderer might not have done it, but how do you prove it?"

"I don't know," I say. "The only proof I have is what I saw in my head, and you're right. To most people that's no proof at all. Except maybe proof that I'm crazy."

The closet door swings open. "I heard talking," Abigail says. "Oh, you have company.

Hello, Adam."

"Uh..hi, Abigail." It always takes Adam a while to relax and feel comfortable around Abigail. It must feel weird to be having a conversation with a cloud of gray mist.

"So what are Holmes and Watson up to this evening?" Abigail asks.

"Studying for a history test. Or trying to," I say.

Abigail picks up my history book and looks at it. "Why, this isn't history! All these things happened long after I was dead!" She frowns. "It's strange to think that history goes on without you."

"'I guess so," I say. "Abigail, I met the man who killed the Jameson sisters. His name is Harold Buchanan."

"And when you met him, you knew he did it, didn't you?"

"Oh, yeah, I knew. But just 'knowing' doesn't do much good when it comes to getting people to believe us. People want proof, and they want to know the reason why somebody committed the crime. We don't have any of that."

"And we don't have any way of getting it either," Adam says.

Abigail perches on top of my dresser. "Oh, I wouldn't be so sure about that."

I close my history book. "What do you mean?"

"Well," Abigail says. "I bet the only way you've tried to gather information so far is by asking questions to the living. I bet you haven't tried to ask questions to the dead." Abigail looks at Adam and me, enjoying the drama. "After all," she says, "Who would be better to talk to than the murder victims themselves?"

"But that's impossible!" Adam says. "You can't just have

conversations with dead people. Uh...I mean, I know I'm having one right now, but Abigail, you're different. These ghosts can't talk, or if they can, I haven't heard them."

"But they can communicate in other ways, can't they?" Abigail says. "They can make knocking sounds, and they left a written message, didn't they?"

Adam nods.

"My mother," Abigail says, twisting one of her ringlets, "was a spiritualist. That is to say, she believed that the living and the dead could communicate with each other. She had a sister, Eugenia, who died in childbirth, and when we lived up East, she used to visit a medium who would help her communicate with Eugenia's spirit. Eugenia couldn't talk, but she could make rapping sounds, and the medium would ask her my mother's questions and tell her to rap once for yes and twice for no. Also...have you ever heard of automatic writing?"

"Is that when you just write down a bunch of stuff without thinking about it?" Adam asks. "I write most of my papers for school that way."

Abigail smiles. "Not exactly. Automatic writing occurs when a spirit possesses a medium'or at least, possesses her hand and the medium writes down a message from the spirit. My mother received several letters from Eugenia that way."

"But how do you know the medium wasn't a fake?" Adam asks.

"I know," Abigail says, "because Mother was reunited with Eugenia after her death. Eugenia remembered every conversation she and Mother had through the medium."

"So you think we can communicate with the Jameson sisters the same way your mom communicated with her sister?" I say.

"Exactly," Abigail says. "We know they can rap and leave messages, so why not?"

Adam's brow is furrowed. "But evidence we get from ghosts is going to sound just as crazy as the evidence we have because Miranda saw the murder in Mr. Buchanan's memories. Nobody is going to believe us."

"Well, not if you go around talking about ghosts," Abigail says, "although why people refuse to believe in us is beyond me. What I thought was that the Jameson sisters might be able to guide you to a source of evidence that people would believe."

"It's worth a shot, I guess," I say. "But where are we going to find a medium?"

Abigail laughs. "Now let me think...who in this room has the Sight and has a proven record of being able to talk to dead people?" Abigail lays a cold hand on my shoulder. "You are a medium, Miranda."

Abigail said we should try to summon the Jameson sisters in whatever room in Adam's house seemed to have the most spiritual activity. Since the living room was out because we couldn't do anything there without Adam's mom noticing, we decided on Adam's bathroom. Since hanging out in the bathroom was an unquestionably weird thing to do, Adam put a movie in the DVD player in his bedroom, turned the volume up a little louder than normal, and closed the bedroom door. That way, he said, if his mom peeked upstairs she'd figure we were watching a movie instead of, say, summoning the dead in the potty room.

We sit down at a little card table we've set up in the bathroom. I'm sitting in a folding chair, but because of limited space, Adam has to sit on the toilet. "I feel like an idiot," he says.

"That makes two of us." I set a sheet of notebook paper and a pen on the table and light a white candle, as Abigail said we should do. I reach over and flip off the light over the sink so that the room is dark except for the candle. "Okay," I say, "Abigail says we have to hold hands'"

"Um...well, you know that if I hold your hand it doesn't mean you're my girlfriend or anything, right? I mean, you're a girl, and you're my friend, but,"

"Adam, it's okay. Go ahead, hold my hands. I promise I won't expect an engagement ring later."

We hold hands across the table, with the candle flickering between us. "Helen and Mildred Jameson," I say. "We summon you from the other world."

Adam snickers. "That sounded really cheesy like a bad horror movie."

"Shh," I say. "Helen and Mildred Jameson, we know Charlie Thomas did not kill you. We know he is innocent."

As soon as I say "he is innocent," the candle's flame waves from side to side like a breeze is blowing it. Adam's hands are starting to sweat. "We want to prove that Charlie Thomas is innocent," I say, "but we need your help. Can you hear me? Rap once if you can hear me, but if you don't mind, rap softly so Adam's mom won't hear it."

For several seconds there is nothing. Then there's a soft knock on the table as if a fist lightly struck it. Adam jumps and loses his grip on my hands, but I grab his hands tighter so our connection won't be broken.

I swallow hard. "Are you the spirit of Mildred Jameson? One rap for yes, two for no."

Rap. Rap.

"Are you the spirit of Helen Jameson? One rap for yes, two for no."

Rap.

"Th-thank you for coming to us, Miss Jameson." It's hard to hold Adam's hands because they're shaking so hard. "Miss Jameson, I think we know the answer to this question, but I want to ask you just to make sure. Did Charlie Thomas kill you and your sister? One rap for yes, two for no."

Rap, rap.

"Okay, good. Now let me ask this. Did Harold Buchanan kill you and your sister?"

Rap.

Adam and I both gasp. When I can talk again, I say, "That was one rap for yes, right?"

Rap.

"I knew it," I say. "I knew it because I saw it in Mr. Buchanan's memories. But Miss Jameson, we don't have any proof that will make people believe us. So if you can tell us anything that might help us, we'd sure appreciate it."

At first there's nothing. No rapping, no movement of the candle flame, no sign that Mildred Jameson is still with us.

But then Adam lets go of my hands, quick. "No!" I hiss. "Don't break the circle!" But then I don't say anything else because I can't say anything else. My mouth is sealed shut, and so are my eyes. If there are any sounds around me, I can't hear them.

And then it happens. My mind clears. It feels blank and empty like a clean sheet of paper. For the first time I can remember, my brain isn't buzzing with other people's thoughts and feelings and with glimpses of what might happen in the future. Instead my brain is floating, at peace, and I feel like I've fallen into a deep, dreamless sleep except that I know I'm awake and sitting across from Adam.

Then, just as suddenly as my mind cleared, it's filled up again. Thoughts and pictures and memories pour back into it just like my brain was an empty glass that's being poured full again. My eyes snap open, and I hear Adam saying, "Miranda, are you okay?" and "You've got to see this!"

"I'm okay," I say. "See what?"

"This." He points to the sheet of paper on the table. The whole page is filled with words.

"Did...did I write this?"

"Yep," Adam says. "With your eyes closed."

I pick up the sheet of paper which is perfumed with a flowery smell it didn't have before, and I look at the neat schoolteacher's handwriting which looks nothing like mine.

"So it worked, did it?" Abigail says as soon as I walk into my room.

"It worked." The sheet of paper is in my hand, and I give it to her and flop down on my bed.

"You look exhausted," Abigail says. "But it's no wonder. Acting as a medium can be quite draining. So you wrote this in a trance?"

"Yeah. I guess you could call it that."

"Hm," Abigail says, frowning down at the paper. So it's a letter from Helen Jameson to Harold Buchanan. Interesting."

"Oh, it's interesting all right," I say. "But it's still not proof. It's another piece of evidence that came right out of my bizarro mind, and the only thing it's going to prove is that I'm a big loony."

"But Miranda," Abigail's tone is gentle, "this letter didn't come out of your mind. It's from Helen Jameson."

"Well, you believe that, and I believe it. But most people seem to be under the impression that dead people can't write letters." I punch my pillow in frustration. "So we've got a letter that explains everything, but nobody will believe it. I don't even know what to do with the thing!"

Abigail looks at me like I'm not too bright. "But it's obvious what you have to do with it. It's a letter from Helen Jameson to Harold Buchanan."

"Yeah? So?"

Abigail places the letter in my hands. "So you have to give it to him."

Chapter Fifteen

"This isn't going to be good," Adam says as we go through the hospital's double doors. "The last time we visited Mr. Buchanan, he didn't exactly invite us to come back."

"And why was that, do you think?" I say. "Could it be because he knows we know he did it?"

Adam shakes his head. "Miranda, since I met you my life's become lots more complicated."

I punch his shoulder. "But it's less boring, isn't it?"

"Yeah, it is, but I don't know...today 'boring' sounds pretty good."

We stand outside Mr. Buchanan's room. When his eyes focus on us, the truth of what he did tears through me again, and it's hard not to double over like somebody just punched me in the stomach.

"You...again?" Mr. Buchanan wheezes.

"Yessir," I say. "We won't bother you for long. We just wanted to bring you something...a letter from a friend of yours."

Mr. Buchanan doesn't want to talk to us, but it's clear I've captured his curiosity.

"Who's it from?" he asks.

I walk toward the bed and hold out the letter. Mr. Buchanan takes it in a pale, trembling hand, then to my surprise, holds it up to his nose. "Evening in Paris," he says.

"I beg your pardon?"

"Evening in Paris," he says, "the perfume. A...a friend of mine used to wear it." He squints down at the letter. "And this is her handwriting! Where...where did you find this?"

I don't want to get into the whole automatic writing thing, so I just say, "We found it in Adam's house. He lives in the old Jameson place."

Mr. Buchanan drops the letter like he's afraid it will burn him.

"Don't you want to read it?" I say.

"The medicine I take..." Mr. Buchanan says, "I can't focus my eyes well enough to read."

I pick up the letter. "Do you want me to read it to you?"

"Well," Mr. Buchanan sighs, "you already know what it says, so I suppose I might as well know, too. Go ahead."

"Close the door, Adam," I whisper. I pull up a chair beside Mr. Buchanan's bed, Adam closes the door, and I start to read:

My dear Harold,

How strange it is that I should call you 'my dear' after what happened! But I suppose you find it stranger still to be receiving a letter from me all these years after my death.

I want you to know that I have never stopped loving you,

even though I have never been quite able to forgive you. Don't misunderstand me. I have forgiven you for killing my sister and me.

What I haven't been able to forgive is the fact that you made an innocent boy pay the price for what you had done. A whole community, all the colored people in Wilder, paid a terrible price, too.

Charlie T was just a child when he went to prison. He was a middle-aged man when they finally set him free, and while he managed to get some of the same things out of life that you did'nt, loving wife and a son, he never did get over what was done to him.

You took Charlie T's life just the same as if you had shot him, too. I understand that you took my life by accident and Mildred's out of anger, but I cannot understand why you took the life of that innocent child, knowing that the sheriff would believe you over him just because you were white and he was colored. That is what I have never been able to forgive.

But that could change. Charlie T is dead now, but even in death his spirit knows no peace.

He is a restless spirit, drifting between the world of the living and the dead, homeless and unable to rest until his problems in the world of the living are solved. Charlie T has gone down in history as a murderer a fact which he feels has hurt his son and his grandchildren and may even hurt his grandchildren's future children. Until Charlie T is proven innocent, he will never be at peace. And Harold, neither will you.

I know that your crime has gnawed at your conscience every day since you committed it. I know this because you are not a bad man. You committed a horrible act out of anger, ambition, and fear, but you are not a bad man. Harold, unless you tell the truth about what happened, you will never know peace, in this world or the next. Since your time in this world is short, this is something you should consider.

There will be no price to pay for your honesty. You will not live long enough to see the inside of a prison cell. and if you make the truth known, you will have my complete forgiveness.

Mildred even says that she will forgive you, too, which is quite something, since she's not the forgiving kind, and since you killed her on purpose. But most importantly, you will be giving Charlie T what he so sorely lacks peace in the knowledge that history will not look upon him as a killer.

My dearest Harold, you know what the right thing is. Please do it. I am asking this out of love.

Yours,
Helen

The whole time I was reading, I kept expecting Mr. Buchanan to stop me, but he just lay there listening like he was hypnotized. Now, when I look up, I see tears in his eyes. "Are you okay?" I ask.

He shakes his head for a second and mutters, "No," then louder says, "No! I don't know if this was something you kids made up for a joke, and then maybe your granny did some conjuring to make the handwriting look like Helen's...and the perfume to smell like Helen's." He wipes away a tear. "I don't know how you did it or why you did it, but I do know it's cruel to torment a dying man."

"But the letter is real," I say softly, trying to sound kind. "She wanted me to give it to you."

Mr. Buchanan isn't listening to me. He's pushing the call button beside his bed and saying, "Nurse, there are children in here disturbing me."

I look at Adam, and Adam looks at me. And we run. We don't stop for breath until we're outside and off hospital property.

"Whew." Adam leans against a tree, gasping. "My dad

would kill me if he ever knew about that."

"Well," I say, rubbing out the sharp pain in my side, "I don't think Mr. Buchanan will say anything to him about it. I don't think he wants to be put in a position where somebody might ask him questions." Adam lets out a little gasp, then covers his eyes and moans, "Oh, no!"

"What?"

"The letter...we forgot it. It's in Mr. Buchanan's room."

"So?"

"So...we'll need it, right? It's evidence."

I throw up my hands. "Evidence of what? That Miranda, that crazy witch girl, thinks ghosts dictate letters to her? Adam, we have no evidence. We have nothing that would prove anything to anybody. We might as well just quit."

Adam jumps in front of where I'm walking. "Quit? But we know who did it!"

"Knowing doesn't make a difference. We've got to have proof. And to normal people, proof that comes from psychic phenomena and voices from the grave just doesn't cut it."

There's nothing else to say. Dejected, we walk through town and to Adam's house. Even though it's chilly, Mrs. So is sitting on the porch. When she see us, she stands up. She does not look happy.

"Uh..hi, Mom," Adam says.

She folds her hands over her chest. "Don't you, hi mom' me, Adam So. I know what you've been up to."

"You...you do?"

I just stand there not sure if I should try to defend Adam or make a run for it.

"Do you know who I just got off the phone with?" Mrs. So says.

Adam looks down at the ground and mumbles, "No, ma'am," but looking into his mind, I see he thinks it was his father, calling because he found out we were bothering Mr. Buchanan.

"Well, I don't know who I was on the phone with either because he didn't tell me his name," Mrs. So says. "I said hello, and this strange voice said, Tell your son to stop asking so many questions, and then he hung up. Adam, you told me you had stopped playing detective!"

"I know, Mom." Adam seems to be finding his Converse high-tops very interesting, since he's not looked up from them. "But we were so close to figuring it out."

Mrs. So puts her hands on her son's shoulders, forcing him to look up at her. "Adam, your father's and my job is to keep you safe. That's why we asked you to stop, and that's why you're stopping now. Do you understand?"

"Yes, ma'am."

"And as punishment for disobeying your father and me, there will be no movies, no video games, and no TV for a full month."

Adam winces but says, "Yes, ma'am."

"Also, after school you must either come directly home or go to your father's office at the hospital. Obviously, you need to stay where we can keep an eye on you." And then she turns to me. "Miranda, I considered waiting to talk to Adam until after you had gone home, but I wanted you to know that you should plan on seeing less of him for the next month. And also, that your detective work has come to an end. I want you to be safe, too, you know." She reaches out and strokes my hair like I'm her daughter.

"Yes, ma'am," I say. "Thank you." I know that we've worried her, and I feel bad.

"Well, Adam," Mrs. So says. "Tell Miranda bye. Since you can't watch movies or play video games, you might as well do some work for me around the house until it's time to start your homework."

"Sheesh," Adam says, once Mrs. So is inside. "She's going to enjoy this." He's trying to sound like he thinks it's funny, but he really sounds like he might cry. "So," he says, "I guess our little adventure is over, huh?" "I guess so." And then I wave and turn away, so he won't see that I really am about to cry.

Chapter Sixteen

"I just feel so guilty," I say, sitting up in bed and hugging my knees to my chest. "Guilty because it was partly my fault we weren't able to help Charlie T...guilty because we let Helen Jameson down."

"You didn't let Helen Jameson down." Abigail looks up from playing the Gameboy Adam loaned her. "You did exactly what she wanted you to. You gave the letter to Harold Buchanan, and since you had no control over how he would respond to it, it's silly to feel guilty. The living waste far too much time feeling guilty. You'll be happy to know that there's no such thing as guilt in the afterlife."

"Well, there's enough in this life to make up for it." I flop back on my bed and stare at the ceiling. "I wish we could go back in time and see if we could figure things out another way."

"Wishes like that are even more useless than guilt," Abigail says, not looking up from her video game. "You know, these little space creatures really are quite difficult to kill. There! Got one!" She looks up at me and smiles.

"Please don't forget to thank Adam for lending me this marvelous machine. I can't remember when I've had such fun."

"Well, I'm glad one of us is having a good time."

Abigail raises an eyebrow at me. "Honestly, Miranda, you can be downright depressing at times. What you need is a good night's sleep. Why don't you go downstairs and make yourself a glass of warm milk? It always used to make me sleepy. You really shouldn't stay up 'til all hours on a school night, fretting about something you can't control."

I look at the clock 12:18. "You're right. Maybe some warm milk would help me relax. It always seems to put baby goats right to sleep."

I tiptoe downstairs and open the refrigerator. The light from the fridge gives the dark kitchen an eerie blue glow. Just as I reach for the milk I hear two sounds that turn my blood to ice water. A crash and a scream. And they both came from my room.

Without even closing the refrigerator, I run up the stairs. When I step into my room, Abigail, who looks pale even for a ghost, says, "Watch where you step. Broken glass is everywhere."

Then I see the reason for the broken glass. The window is shattered, and in the middle of the floor is a rock a little larger than a baseball. "Somebody threw it at the window," Abigail says. "It went right through my head."

I want to examine the rock more closely, but I'm afraid to walk across the floor barefoot.

"Can you hand me the rock?" I ask Abigail.

She glides right over the broken glass, picks up the rock, and places it in my hand. It's then I notice that it's not just a rock. A piece of paper has been tied to it with thick twine. I pull out the paper, unfold it, and read the words that have been typed on it:

STOP ASKING SO MANY QUESTIONS. I feel like I'm going to be sick.

"What's going on?"

I turn around to see Mom in her blue kimono and Granny right behind her in her high-necked black gown.

There's no point in lying. "Somebody threw a rock at my window. It went right through Abigail's head."

Mom gasps. "Well, it was lucky it was Abigail standing by the window and not you. A rock that big could've knocked you out cold."

"Or killed you deader than a mackerel," Granny adds.

Mom shoots Granny an annoyed glance. "Thank you, Mother. That was comforting." Then her eyes are on the paper in my hand. "Show me that note."

I hand it to her.

"So this is about the snooping around you've been doing about the Jameson place," she says.

It's not a question, so I don't answer her.

"I told you to quit that, Miranda," Granny says. "I told you it was dangerous."

"Yes, ma'am," I say. "And you were right."

Mom runs her hand over the note. "A young man wrote this...a boy, really, somebody close to your age, Miranda. And he was the one who tied it to the rock and threw it, too. Here, Mother, see what you can sense about this."

Granny closes her eyes and runs her hand over the note, too. "You're right, Sarah. It was a boy that wrote the note and throwed the rock. But he was doing it on somebody else's orders...somebody older and more powerful."

"They're good," Abigail says.

"I know," I whisper.

"So," Mom says, "I suppose I should call the sheriff's

office."

"Sarah, sometimes you ain't got the sense God give a goose," Granny says. "Since when has anybody in the sheriff's office believed a word anybody in this family said? The sheriff we got now and his daddy before him both thought you and me murdered our husbands with magic but covered it up so we wouldn't get caught. The sheriff'd say we broke the window ourselves while we was trying to cast some spell to conjure the devil."

"You're right," Mom sighs. "But Miranda, I want you to promise me that to stay safe, you'll follow the advice on this note. Somebody wants you to stop asking questions, and this somebody is willing to hurt you to make you stop."

"I...I've already stopped," I say.

"Okay," Mom says, and I can tell she sees I'm telling the truth. "Well, why don't you spend the rest of the night in my room? I can do a better job cleaning up all this glass when I can see it in daylight."

"And I reckon I might stay up a little longer and look into some ways to protect Miranda from whoever it is that's out to get her."

"Okay, Mother," Mom says, rolling her eyes.

"Roll your eyes all you want, Missy," Granny says. "But I can do a dang sight better than the Wilder Sheriff's Department keeping this house safe."

At breakfast Granny presents me with a little cheesecloth bag attached to a silk cord. Whatever is inside the bag smells horrible'like rotting cabbage and onions.

"Wear that bag around your neck," Granny says. "It'll keep you safe."

"Why?" I say, holding my nose. "Because I'll stink so bad nobody'll get close enough to hurt me?"

Granny ignores me and hands me a second bag. "This one's for your little Oriental friend. He needs protection, too."

On my way to school I take the bag from around my neck and stuff it, along with Adam's, inside my backpack. Even though my backpack is zipped shut, I can still smell the stinky herbs.

Before home room, I walk up to Adam at his locker and say, "Hey, my granny made you a present."

I toss him the bag. As soon as the smell hits him, he crinkles his nose and sticks his tongue out. "Eww! It smells like when my mom makes kimchee."

"Well, according to Granny, it's for your protection. I have one, too. I guess Granny got a little worried after somebody threw a rock through my window last night."

"What?" Adam's eyebrows shoot up in surprise.

"The rock went straight through Abigail's head. There was a note attached to it that said the same thing the guy who called your house said on the phone."

"Whoa." Adam looks at the bag. "Maybe I should wear this thing after all. So...do you think that since we have stopped asking questions whoever it is will stop bothering us?"

"Yeah," I say. "I'm not worried. But I have to admit it sort of bothers me...giving the bad guys what they want."

"I know," Adam says, "but real life isn't like the movies. Sometimes the bad guys win."

I'm in history class listening to Mrs. Harris talk about the knights in the Middle Ages when an announcement comes over the intercom: "Miranda Jasper, report to the office, please. Miranda Jasper, report to the office."

When most kids get called to the office the other kids

in class say, "Ooh!" to joke about somebody getting in trouble. But nobody says anything when I get up to leave the room.

When I walk up to the desk of Mrs. Wheeler, the old lady who's the school secretary, I say, "Uh...hi. You called me on the intercom."

She looks up over her half-glasses which she wears on a chain. She is thinking, "It always makes me nervous to talk to the little witch girl," but what she says is, "You've got a phone call, honey."

"A phone call?" Here my Sight is failing me. I have no idea who could be calling me unless it's the person who called Adam's mother yesterday. Mrs. Wheeler holds out the receiver, and I take it and say, "Hello?"

"She came to me last night."

It's a man's voice, but it's soft and shaky, and for a second I have a hard time figuring out who it is. "Mr. Buchanan?"

"Yes. It was Helen. She came to me. We...talked. I need to see you today, Miranda. What time can you be here?"

I'm having a hard time taking in everything he's saying... that he and Helen somehow talked, that he wants to talk to me. "I guess three-thirty is the earliest I could get over there."

"All right...three-thirty. Bring your friend, too."

Then there's a click and a dial tone. I hand the phone back to Mrs. Wheeler, and I must look strange because she says, "Are you all right, honey?"

"Yes, ma'am." I start back to history class, but I know I'm not going to be paying much attention to my teacher's talk about knights and chivalry. What's going on in the present is far more interesting.

Back in class, I slip Adam a note. It says:

OK, this is weird. Mr. Buchanan says Helen came and talked

*to him last night. He wants to talk to us today at 3:30. I know
you're in trouble at home, but can you be there?*

There's no need for Adam to pass a note back. He just
makes eye contact with me, and I read his thoughts: *Are you
kidding? Of course I'll be there.*

Chapter Seventeen

Adam is waiting in the hall outside Mr. Buchanan's room at 3:25. I'm nervous'nervous about what Mr. Buchanan is going to say and nervous that Adam is going to get into even more trouble for being here with me. "Are you sure it's okay for you to be doing this?" I ask.

"Sure I'm sure," he says. "I checked in with Dad when I got here, and he slipped me a five and told me to get a snack in the cafeteria and stay out of trouble." He grins. "Dad doesn't keep anywhere near as close an eye on me as Mom thinks he does."

"Well, I'm not sure what you're about to do is exactly staying out of trouble."

Adam shrugs. "Dad likes me to keep the patients company when they're lonely. And Mr. Buchanan did invite us."

"That's true." I look at the clock on the wall. "Are you ready?"

"Unless he's got a gun hidden under his pillow, I'm ready

for him."

I smile, but Adam's words haven't done much to settle my nerves. I knock lightly on Mr. Buchanan's propped-open door.

"Children," he says. "Come in." He is propped up in bed, looking even thinner and paler than the last time we saw him. "Miranda." He looks at me, and like always, I feel the pain he has caused other people rip through me. "Will you get me some water from that pitcher, please?"

"Yessir." I pour the water from the plastic pitcher and hold the cup while he sucks through a straw.

"Thank you," he says, out of breath. "I'm glad you two got here on time, children. We have another visitor who's coming in about fifteen minutes, but I've got a lot to tell you before he gets here...things that only the two of you would believe." He lets out a hollow cough, then says, "Why don't you pull up some chairs and sit next to my bed? I don't have the strength to talk loud, so it's better if you're close."

"Yessir." Adam and I scoot chairs up to Mr. Buchanan's bed and sit down so close we're almost touching him. The feeling of death that surrounds him makes me sick and dizzy'both the deaths he has caused and his own approaching death, which hangs over his head like a poison black cloud.

"Last night," Mr. Buchanan says, "I was lying in bed awake, as usual. Since I found out I'm dying, I've had a hard time sleeping. It's almost as if my body knows it's heading toward eternal sleep, so it wants to stay awake for as long as possible before that happens."

"Yessir," I say because he's stopped to take a breath.

"So," Mr. Buchanan continues, "there I was, awake. I want to make it clear I was awake so you'll know I wasn't dreaming. And then I heard somebody come into the room. I figured it was the nurse coming in to check my blood pressure or some such. It's a wonder anybody gets any sleep in a hospital, as many nurses as they send in at night to pester you." He stares off in the distance for a second. "But when I turned my head to see who it was, it wasn't a nurse at all. It was Helen." His voice is shaky, and his eyes are wet. "The smell of her perfume filled the air, and there she was, looking just like she'd looked in 1934...in that blue dotted dress I'd always liked, her soft brown curls like a little cap on her head, those pretty blue eyes looking at me through her glasses...looking at me like she was looking through me, just like she used to all those years ago. She walked right up to the side of my bed, said 'Harold,' and then she reached out and stroked my hair. It felt...not like somebody's hand, but like...like."

"A cool breeze blowing through your hair," I say, thinking of Abigail.

He looks surprised. "Yes. Yes, exactly like that. She said she'd come to tell me that the letter was real...that she'd written it herself through you. But you should have known it was real in the first place, she said, 'unless you've forgotten my handwriting and my perfume?' I told her I hadn't forgotten, and she smiled and said she hadn't forgotten anything about me either. But the way she said it, I could tell she was remembering the bad as well as the good. I told her I wished she could forget some things, and she shook her head and said that she couldn't forget, but she could forgive. 'But,' she said, 'I can only forgive you if you make a full confession.'

Mr. Buchanan closes his eyes for a second, like he's lost in a memory. When he starts talking again, it's almost like he's in a trance. "She stroked my hair again, then said, 'Take my hand, Harold. I want you to feel something.' I took her hand, and my hand was surrounded by coolness. Then a wave of pain washed over me. But pain is too weak a word to describe it. It hurt more than cancer, more than any pain you could ever imagine. My body was in agony, but my body and mind felt even worse like I was alone and betrayed. This is when I die, I thought. I have to die now because nobody can be in this much pain and live. But then she let go of my hand, and that second the pain was gone.

"What was that?" I said, wiping tears from my eyes. She said, 'Do you remember back in school, when I taught you about fractions?' I said I remembered a little about fractions, yes.

She said, "Well, here's a fraction for you: the pain that you just felt was one-one millionth of the pain you caused the day Mildred and I died. And the worst pain wasn't even Mildred's and mine that was over in seconds. Charlie's pain went on for years and years...it's still going on today.' She said, 'Harold, I beg you to make amends before it's too late. You'll only cause more pain to yourself and others if you don't.' Then she told me she loved me and leaned in to kiss me. I closed my eyes to kiss her back. I felt a cool breeze on my lips, and when I opened my eyes, she was gone."

He is quiet for a few seconds, then he says, "So the letter wasn't a prank, was it?"

"No, sir," I say.

"Did you see her when you wrote it?" Mr. Buchanan asks me.

"No, sir. I didn't see her or anything else. It was like I wasn't even there."

"I watched her write the letter," Adam says. "She wrote the whole thing with her eyes closed. It was freaky."

Harold shakes his head. "I never thought such things were possible."

"Granny always says there's a lot more going on in the

world than most people realize," I tell him. "People just don't open up their eyes to see it."

"Yes," Harold says. "I suppose that's true." He breathes a tired sigh. "And that's what I wanted to tell you before our other guest gets here. I knew that if I tried to tell him that part of the story, he wouldn't believe it or anything else I told him. He'd think I was just a sick old man whose mind had turned to jelly. Miranda, may I have another drink of water?"

"Of course." I hold the cup for him. He drinks a few swallows, then stops when another visitor walks up to the door. When I see who it is, I almost spill the cup.

Tom Franklin, the sheriff of Wilder County, waddles through the door. He's dressed in his tan uniform (which must be in extra-extra-extra large size), but he holds his hat in his hands.

Adam looks at the sheriff's badge, then looks at me, his mouth hanging open.

"Howdy, Mr. B. You was wanting to talk to me?" Sheriff Franklin sounds friendly but a little confused about why he's been called here.

"Yes, Tom, thank you for coming," Mr. Buchanan says. "There's something I need to tell you...and these children. Why don't you have a seat?"

"Well...all right." The sheriff sounds puzzled, but sits down like he's been asked to.

"Adam," Mr. Buchanan says, "there's a tape recorder on the bedside table. Will you hit the record button, please? I think Tom might like to have a record of this conversation."

Adam hits the record button.

"So, Tom," Mr. Buchanan says, almost cheerfully, "have you ever heard of what's called a deathbed confession?"

"Yessir," the sheriff says. "I've heard of something like that."

"Well," Mr. Buchanan says, "what you're about to hear is a deathbed confession. Many years ago...many years before you were even born, Tom, back when your daddy was still a baby...I did something very wrong." He stops to catch his breath for a second, then says, "I did something very wrong, and I've never admitted it until now. But my time in the world is not long, and I can't die with this black spot on my conscience."

"Well, then, Mr. Buchanan," the sheriff says kindly, "you tell me what you want to tell me."

"The Trojan War was started because of a woman named Helen," Mr. Buchanan says. "And the war I've been fighting inside myself for seventy years was also caused by a woman named Helen. Helen Jameson."

Sheriff Bailey scoots to the edge of his seat. "You mean Helen Jameson like the Jameson sisters?"

"Yes, that Helen Jameson. She and I," He looks at Adam and me, "loved each other."

"Hm," Sheriff Franklin says, "wasn't she a quite a bit older than you?"

"Yes." Mr. Buchanan is smiling, but it's a sad kind of smile. "There were fifteen years between us, and that was one of our biggest problems. It didn't bother either of us, but we knew it would be a problem in town. I had been Helen's student once upon a time, although our romance didn't start until the summer after I graduated from high school. Even so, Helen knew that if word got out about her seeing a young man who had once been her student, she'd lose her job. People back then probably would have accepted a male teacher seeing a young woman who had once been his student, but a schoolmarm with an eighteen-year-old boy? It would have been a scandal."

Sheriff Franklin smooths his moustache. "I reckon so. I've known lesser things than that to set jaws to flapping in this town."

"Exactly," Mr. Buchanan says. "And then, too, we had my ambitions to consider. My daddy was on the city council and wanted me to follow in his footsteps and maybe even move on to a position in the state or national government. I had graduated at the top of my high school class and had been awarded a full scholarship to UK. My future was rolled out in front of me like a red carpet. Miranda, another sip of water, please."

He sips, then says, "But Helen was my secret. From my parents, from my friends. Nobody knew about us because we would both have too much to lose if anybody found out. And yet our hearts belonged to each other. After many serious talks we decided that I should go off to UK and that we would write each other every day. Then after I graduated from college, I would come back to Wilder, a grown man of twenty-two, and then Helen and I could start seeing each other publicly. After a few months of letting the town get used to us as a couple, we would get married. That was the plan."

"But something got in the way of your plan?" the sheriff asks.

"Someone, actually," Mr. Buchanan says. "Mildred. Helen's sister."

I remember Abigail's nickname for Mildred: Mil-dread. And I remember Granny saying Helen was always sweet, but Mildred was always sour. "I heard," I say, "that Mildred was kind of hard to get along with."

To my surprise, Mr. Buchanan laughs. "Well, honey, whoever described her to you that way was being awfully polite. I've never seen two family members as opposite as Helen and Mildred Jameson. It was like Helen was everything I ever loved, and Mildred was everything I ever—" He stops before he finishes the sentence, then finally says, "Mildred was hard to get along with."

"Was she mean?" Adam asks.

"Yes, son, she was mean," Mr. Buchanan says. "The way she treated Helen was terrible.

Always telling her she was ugly and she had no common sense. 'An educated fool,' she used to call Helen. And she made Helen work so hard! Helen taught school from eight to three five days a week. The only job Mildred had was giving piano lessons to the few kids who weren't too scared of her to take them, which she did for three hours a week at the very most. It would seem fair that if Helen was doing most of the work and earning most of the money, Mildred would pitch in and do some of the work around the house. But no! She expected Helen to do all the housework and cooking. I used to call her my little Cinderella. Once Helen suggested that they hire a girl to come in once a week and help with the cleaning, but Mildred told Helen that not only was she the laziest person on earth, she was also a spendthrift who would squander every cent of their money if Mildred wasn't there to watch her."

"Wow," I say, "why did Helen keep on living with Mildred if she treated her so badly?"

Harold smiles. "Because she was so sweet. Helen was a victim of her own kindness. She said that with their parents dead, Mildred was the only family she had, and that family had to stick together. She said she would move out of the family home once we got married, but until then she would stay with Mildred because she did love her, even though she made her cry sometimes." He shakes his head like he's shaking off a bad memory. "Mildred made her cry quite often, actually."

The sheriff looks up from cleaning his fingernails with a pocket knife. "Don't get me wrong here, Mr. Buchanan, this is a real interestin' story. But I don't understand what it is you felt like you needed to tell me. If this has something to do with the Jameson sisters' murder, that case was solved as soon as it happened."

"I'm getting to the part I need to tell you," Mr. Buchanan says. "I just want to make sure I explain myself so you'll understand why I did what I did...although sometimes I'm not so sure I understand it myself."

He gestures for another drink, and I give it to him.

After he swallows, he says, "As you might imagine, it was hard for Helen and me to see each other. We couldn't be seen together in public, and it was hard to see each other in private because I still lived with my parents, and they kept a close eye on me. And Mildred kept an even closer eye on Helen, even though Helen was a grown woman and should have been able to do as she pleased. The one time a week Helen and I could always see each other was Tuesday afternoons. Mildred had a Ladies Missionary Circle meeting that she never missed, which meant that Helen and I could have an hour and a half together while Mildred was away. I lived for that hour and a half a week."

Mr. Buchanan looks like he might smile from the memories, but then something stops him short. "Helen and I would sit on the couch in the living room and talk and hold hands, kiss a little, and the time would pass like it was just a few seconds." He takes a deep breath. "Well, one Tuesday afternoon, the day of the murders, Helen and I were sitting on the couch as usual. I had just leaned in for a kiss, my eyes were closed, and I guess Helen's were too, when I heard a scream. I opened my eyes, and I saw Mildred standing there with the black boy everybody called Charlie T, and she was screaming like she had seen me attacking Helen instead of just kissing her."

"Hm," the sheriff says, putting his knife back in his pants pocket, "Do you reckon she was screaming because Charlie T was threatening her or hurting her some way?"

"No," Mr. Buchanan says. "Charlie T wasn't doing a thing but carrying his newspaper bag. I guess he was out delivering papers, and Mildred saw him on her way home and invited him in to do a chore of some kind. They paid Charlie T to do their yard work and fix little things around the house...the 'man's work' they didn't know anything about. So Charlie T was just standing there frozen while Mildred screamed and screamed." Mr. Buchanan winces like he can still hear the screaming. "Helen got up off the couch and went to try to calm Mildred down. She put her hands on Mildred's shoulders and said,'Let me explain...if you'll just calm down, I'll explain everything.'"

Mr. Buchanan shakes his head. "But Mildred said there was nothing to explain, that she knew what she saw. Then she said, 'Harold Buchanan, I am going to call your parents and tell them about this,' but even worse, she said to Helen, 'And won't the principal and the school board be interested to hear about how dear old Miss Jameson is carrying on with one of her students?' Well, Helen just got hysterical. She begged Mildred not to tell, and said, 'Harold's out of school, and he's not been my student for years. I'd get fired if you told, and we need my salary.' But Mildred said they could get by on the money their daddy left them. 'It would be tight,' she said, but I remember she said, 'some things are more important than money things like keeping a scarlet woman like you away from innocent schoolchildren!'

Harold's forehead wrinkles, as if the memory causes him physical pain. "I jumped up then, and said, 'Now wait a minute, Mildred.' But she said she would not wait, that somebody needed to be in charge here. The tone of her voice changed; it sounded almost kind. 'Harold, Helen,' she said, 'I will consider not telling either the Buchanans or the school officials about this if you two will meet certain conditions.' Helen asked what the conditions were, as innocent as a babe in the woods. Mildred said the first condition was that Helen and I never see each other again and if we did happen to run into each other on the street, we were to pass without speaking. Well, about this time Charlie T finally found his voice and said he'd best be going and he'd come back another day about that yard work. But Mildred yelled, 'No! Stay, Charlie ! I want you to witness this. And there'll be some money in this for you to make sure you keep quiet about what you saw.' And of course, the times being what they were, there wasn't anything for Charlie T to do but say 'yes ma'am' and stay put.

"Then Mildred turned back to Helen. She said, 'The second condition is this: you're going to start living your life according to what I would like. You can go to your job as usual, but once you're home, you will spend your time doing exactly what I tell you to do. If I want you to scrub the bathroom with a toothbrush, you do it. If I want you to get out of bed at one o'clock in the morning and bake me a cake, you'll do it. Do you know why you'll do it?" Mr. Buchanan's eyes are wet with tears. "By this time Helen was crying so hard she could barely say no. But when she did, Mildred smiled, and it was the ugliest smile I'd ever seen. She said, 'Because if you don't, I'll tell.' I told Mildred that she couldn't do that, that it was blackmail, but she said, 'Don't tell me what I can and cannot do.' Then she slapped Helen's face hard, so hard she knocked her glasses off, and called her a name that's not fit to say in front of children."

Mr. Buchanan sighs. "That's when I snapped. You have to understand. I was young, I was crazy in love, and I thought I was rescuing the woman I loved from peril. I knew, because Helen had showed it to me, that their father's pistol was sitting on the mantle behind the clock. They were always a little scared of intruders and kept it for protection. And of course, I thought I was using the gun for protection, too, when I grabbed it and stood face to face with Mildred, pointing it at her.

'Don't you ever talk to Helen like that,' I said. 'I'm going to settle this here and now.' Like I said, I was young, and I thought I was the hero in a cowboy movie. But I swear I never planned to shoot Mildred, just to scare her.

"But then Helen screamed, 'No!' and tried to grab the gun from my hands. We struggled with it for a couple of seconds, like a tug of war, and I don't know which one of us accidentally pulled the trigger, but the gun went off." Mr. Buchanan's eyes spill over with tears. "She was shot through the heart. The heart that had belonged to me. She died...instantly."

"Now wait a minute, Mr. B." The sheriff is on his feet now, pacing. "Are you telling me that Charlie Thomas didn't kill Helen Jameson'that you did, by accident?"

"Yes," Mr. Buchanan says, his voice still choked from crying. "Helen's death was an accident. But Mildred's death was not."

The sheriff's jaw drops. "You killed Mildred Jameson, too?"

"Yes." Mr. Buchanan looks the sheriff straight in the eye. "As soon as Helen fell to the floor, Mildred started screaming,

'You killed her! You killed her! Murderer! Murderer!' I had just lost the only person I loved, and standing before me, alive and screaming, was the only person I hated. I was so filled with rage I didn't even think. I just pulled the trigger."

"And Charlie T was just standing there the whole time," I say.

"Yes," Mr. Buchanan says. "Some people run when they're scared, and some people freeze on the spot. Charlie T froze. His face was frozen in this look of horror...he looked more like a statue than a person. And as I saw him there, I realized he was a witness to the murder I'd just committed. I held the gun on him, but the horror of what I had just done was sinking in, and my finger wouldn't touch the trigger."

Mr. Buchanan closes his eyes and takes a deep breath. "It's this next part that's the hardest to talk about. Still holding the gun, I checked Helen's pulse to make double sure she was dead. There was no need to check Mildred's pulse...just looking at her you knew there was no way she could be alive. And then I did the worst thing I've ever done.

"I looked at Charlie T standing there, and suddenly the whole future that had been spread out before me was in danger of disappearing. I couldn't let my dreams be destroyed because of one accidental killing and one justifiable one, I thought. I had a full scholarship to go to UK the next month. I was going to be a successful business man, a politician, a leader in my community. I kept looking at Charlie T. In a time and place like that, I thought, what future could a black kid like him have? His opportunities were so limited that he'd be doing odd jobs and yard work for the rest of his life. And that was when I made the coldest, most selfish decision of my life. I decided that my future was more valuable than Charlie T's."

"But...but you couldn't have known that," I say. "You can't just decide one person's life means more than another's."

"I know that now," Mr. Buchanan says. "But at the time I was full of the arrogance of youth, and I truly believed I had more to offer the world than a boy like Charlie T did. So I held the gun on him, and I said, 'You did this, do you understand?' He said, No sir. So I repeated, 'You did this. You killed the Jameson sisters because you were mad that they paid some other boy to do their yard work for them.'"

Mr. Buchanan pulls up the cover on his bed like he's suddenly cold. "Charlie T was shaking and crying like a child, which is, of course, what he was. He tried to interrupt me...he said, 'But Mr. Buchanan,' and I said' But, nothing. When the sheriff gets here, you confess to the murder. You'll do some jail time, but I tell you what. If you tell the sheriff what really happened, I've got friends who'll make sure you don't live long enough to say another word. So what are you gonna tell them, boy?' I said. Charlie T was crying so hard he barely choked out, 'I did it.'

I said, 'That's right. You did it,' and that's when I grabbed the poker from the fireplace and knocked him out cold. I cleaned my fingerprints off the gun and put it in Charlie T's hand. And then I called the sheriff's office and said that I'd heard screams and shots coming from the Jameson place. I said I'd run in to find Charlie T holding a gun over the dead bodies of the Jameson sisters and that I'd managed to sneak up behind him and knock him out with a poker. I didn't give the sheriff my name, and as soon as I hung up the phone, I got out of there and ran straight home."

The sheriff has taken off his glasses and is rubbing his eyes like he has a killer headache. "Mr. Buchanan," he says, "are you sure it happened like you say it did?"

"Of course I'm sure. It's my body that's failing, not my mind."

"Hm," the sheriff says. "What was it that made you want to confess after all these years?"

"Well," Mr. Buchanan says, turning to look at Adam and me. "These young people were part of it. They're the ones who figured out I did it."

"You two?" The sheriff sounds like what he just heard is even more shocking than Mr. Buchanan confessing to murder.

"Yessir," I say. "Adam here lives in the old Jameson place, and that got us interested in the murder, so we did some research and went around asking people questions."

"I heard they were asking questions," Mr. Buchanan says. "My buddy Roy Silcox came over one day and told me a couple of kids had come to his office asking about the Jameson murder. He told me this not knowing I was the one who did it, of course, but just by way of making conversation. He said the girl was Irene Chandler's spooky little granddaughter, and the boy was Chinese."

"Korean," Adam says so softly that only I can hear him.

"I got worried," Mr. Buchanan says, "so I got my great grandson Cody who goes to school with these kids to leave some notes and even make an anonymous phone call to Adam's house, telling them to stop snooping."

"Cody Taylor is your great-grandson?" Adam says. "He's such a pain!"

Mr. Buchanan smiles. "He can be, yes. And I shouldn't have encouraged him to harass you."

"Oh, Cody doesn't need encouragement," I say. "He harasses us all the time."

"Well, I apologize just the same," Mr. Buchanan says.

"So what was it that made you decide to come clean?" the sheriff asks.

"Well," Mr. Buchanan looks at me. "It was because of a visitor I had."

"A visitor?" the sheriff asks.

I look Mr. Buchanan in the eye, trying to send him the message: Please don't tell him about Helen visiting you from the other side.

"Yes," Mr. Buchanan says. "I was visited by my conscience. It...spoke to me."

"Well," the sheriff says, popping the tape out of the tape recorder. "I hope you feel better getting this all off your chest. But I've got to tell you, from a legal standpoint, there's not a thing we can do about this. I remember reading in the paper a few years back that Charlie T died. And there were no witnesses to the crime that we can call on. And even if there was, what would be the point? Your health isn't good enough for you to go through a trial, let alone serve time in jail." The sheriff pats Mr. Buchanan on the shoulder. "After all the good things you've done for this town over the years, Mr. B, it seems like it might be best if what you just said in this room stays in this room."

"No!" Mr. Buchanan says with more force than you'd think somebody so old and sick could muster. "Don't you see? No matter how much good I did later, I still killed two women and ruined one man's life. And what about all the other people I hurt? All the innocent people who got run out of town because of my lies? This secret has tortured me for seventy years, Tom. It has to come out in the open so I'll be free and so that the little Thomas children will know their granddaddy wasn't a murderer."

The sheriff shakes his head. "Well, I reckon I could run over to the district attorney's office and see what he has to say about it. You're sure that's what you want, Mr. B?"

"I'm sure."

"Well, all right then." The sheriff stops in the doorway. "A seventy year old murder case solved by a couple of grade schoolers, and one of the biggest bigwigs in Wilder begging to tell the world he's the murderer. It's been an interesting day."

I look at Mr. Buchanan. Now that he's told the truth, I can look at him without feeling pain. "That was brave," I say.

"Yeah," Adam agrees.

"No," Mr. Buchanan says. His face looks drawn, tired. "If I was brave I would've told the truth seventy years ago."

"But the sheriff offered to keep the whole thing quiet, and you told him not to. That was brave."

"Nope," Mr. Buchanan says. "I was just afraid of what would happen to me in the next life if I didn't let the truth come out. Helen told me it wouldn't be pretty." He yawns. "You know what? For the first time in a long time, I feel like I could really sleep."

"Well," Adam says, "we should go and let you rest, then."

"Yes," Mr. Buchanan says. "Would you close the curtains and turn out the lights first?"

Adam pulls down the shades, and I dim the lights. On my way out the door I turn back to say goodbye to Mr. Buchanan, but he is already asleep.

Chapter Eighteen

Today's my birthday. I don't know how being twelve will be, but the last couple of months being eleven were pretty exciting. Thanks to the district attorney and Mr. Buchanan's son, Senator Harold Buchanan III, the governor agreed to pardon Charlie Thomas for the murder of the Jameson sisters. The governor said he wasn't in the habit of pardoning dead people, but that Charlie T had obviously been a victim of the times he lived in. As soon as the pardon came through, Charlie Thomas Junior sent Adam and me a whole sweet potato pie and a note saying he was going to frame the pardon and hang it in his restaurant.

Something else happened when the pardon came through. The handprints on the living room wall disappeared. There was one final message on the bathroom mirror, though. Adam saw the words one night when he was getting out of the shower: *He is at peace.*

Mr. Buchanan is at peace, too. He died in his sleep a few days after he confessed to the murder.

When Roy Silcox told Adam and me that he'd put us on the front page of the newspaper if we solved the case, he probably never guessed he'd have to make good on his promise. But if you look at last week's *Wilder Herald*, you'll see Adam and me, as big as life, along with pictures of the Jameson place and Helen, Mildred, and Charlie T.

Somebody in Lexington must have gotten a look at the *Herald*, too, because yesterday a pretty reporter and a camera crew came all the way here to interview Adam and me for the TV news. The reporter talked to Granny, too, and thought she was so interesting that she's going to come back and do a story just about Granny as part of a series about Appalachian folk life. I wonder if the fact that she's going to be on TV will make Granny finally break down and agree to buy one. I probably shouldn't get my hopes up.

And so tonight, for my birthday, Adam and I are sitting in my room with a bowl of popcorn in front of the little portable TV Adam has brought over, getting ready to watch ourselves on the news. Abigail is sitting as close to the TV as she can get without blocking our view. "Just look!" she cries, staring at the screen and clasping her hands together. "Isn't it wonderful?"

"It's just a Burger King commercial," Adam says.

The news comes on, and there is a shot of downtown Wilder and the Jameson place. Then we see old photos of the Jameson sisters, Charlie T, and Harold Buchanan. Then there's Adam and me, looking at the microphone in front of our faces like it's going to bite us. Abigail squeals when she sees us on the screen, and Adam says, "Ugh, I shouldn't have worn that shirt. It makes me look diseased."

"Shh," I hiss, so I can hear the reporter ask, "So how did you, a couple of grade-school kids, figure out that the police had been wrong about a seventy-year-old case?"

I watch us stand there looking terrified until Adam says, "Well...uh, I know a lot about searching for information on the internet and stuff, and my mom helped some, too."

"And you, Miranda?" the reporter asks.

I watch myself think for a second, then say, "Well... sometimes I just have a...a sense about people. Oh, and my friend Abigail helped some, too."

Abigail shrieks and wraps her cold arms around me. "I can't believe you said my name on television! I'm famous!"

I shush Abigail long enough to hear the reporter finish by saying, "...a seventy-yeear-old wrong righted by a pair of precocious sixth graders."

For a second I'm sad because I know we didn't right the wrong done against Charlie T. What good does it do to prove somebody innocent after he's already dead? But Abigail reads my thoughts and says, "You still helped him. You set his spirit free."

"You're right," I say. "Thank you."

"Thank you for what?" Adam says.

"I was thanking Abigail for what she just said," I tell him.

"But Abigail didn't say anything." Adam is looking at me like I've lost my mind.

"But she did."

"No," Abigail interrupts me. "I didn't say anything out loud. I was talking to you silently, in your head, and you heard me."

"Really?" I'm shocked. "I've never been able to do that before."

Abigail smiles. "You're another year older, Miranda. Your powers are getting stronger."

She's right. I feel like a door's been unlocked in my brain, and I know everything that's behind it. I know that Adam and Abigail and I will stay friends and have more adventures together. I know that Granny will be upstairs soon carrying a homemade apple stack cake with twelve birthday candles. And I know that Mom will be right behind her, carrying a big present wrapped in purple tissue paper. And I won't have to unwrap it to know what's inside.

Bean Pole Books
A Division of Southern Belle Books
PO Box 242
Midway, Florida 32343

www.BeanPoleBooks.net